BEECH BANK GIRLS III

Beech Bank Girls III

Christmas Is Coming!

ELEANOR WATKINS

DERNIER PUBLISHING

Tonbridge

Book design and production for the publisher by
Bookprint Creative Services, <www.bookprint.co.uk>
Printed in Great Britain

To the two newest
girls in my family, great-niece Maddison
and great-great-niece Samantha,
with love

Contents

PART ONE

Holly's Story

COMING HOME

one

The first thing that grabbed me when we touched down at Heathrow was the greyness. It made me shiver just looking at it. Grey skies, the kind that my dad says mean there's snow coming soon. Grey airport buildings, people scurrying about in grey clothes (well, of course, they weren't all grey, but after the bright jazzy stuff I'd seen people wearing lately they all *seemed* grey). And cold, once we got into the open air. The kind of horrid damp chill that creeps into your bones. I shivered and pulled my denim jacket closer round me as we climbed into the taxi that was taking us home.

"I did advise you to wear something warm, didn't I?" said Mum, in her told-you-so kind of voice. "It's winter here, you know."

"Yeah, yeah," I said grumpily. She had told me, over and over, when we were packing to come home. But I just couldn't picture it. It was hot and getting hotter, back there in Oz, and for six weeks I'd lived in shorts, suntops and flip-flops, or a bikini. I'd seemed to have forgotten what a British winter is really like. Now I felt definitely under-dressed, in my jeans, top and thin jacket.

It was a bit warmer in the car with the heater on. I leaned my head against the headrest and yawned. It had been a long, long flight, and I knew I'd be jet-lagged. I watched the dreary, grey streets and later the damp, leafless countryside and thought of the wide golden beaches, the blue sea, the brilliant coloured birds and butterflies I'd seen, the exotic scenery, the sun always shining. And the people.

I felt a tear squeeze from between my eyelids when I thought of my cousin Sarah, who lived in Australia all the time now and who I wouldn't see again for ages. Sarah and I have twin sisters for our mothers and we've always been as close as sisters ourselves. And the friends we'd both made and the fun we'd had – beach barbies, swimming and snorkelling with the youth group from Sarah's church, shopping and sightseeing and hanging out. I remembered the times we'd had singing round a bonfire on the beach after dark, with one of the guys playing a guitar and sparks flying up to meet the stars. I was going to miss them all so badly. Talking on Chatspace or even Skype just wouldn't be the same.

I must have dozed a bit, because the scenery was beginning to look familiar and I realised we weren't that far from home.

"Soon be there now," said Mum.

"I hope the heating's on," I said.

"It will be," said Mum. "I took care to arrange all that. It'll be good to be home – what a journey! And to sleep in our own beds."

She was trying to cheer me up and jolly me along, but I was already having a hard job of it getting used to the idea of being back in the grey old UK, and I didn't care who knew it.

We were coming into town now, and it was getting dark, and lights were coming on in the houses.

"You'll love seeing all your friends again," said Mum. "They'll want to hear everything you've been doing. And everybody at the Beech Bank Club. Talking of which – isn't that Chloe and Rachel on their way there now?"

We were passing the long low building that used to be the old community centre and is now the headquarters of the Beech Bank Club, a cool after-school place run by our vicar and his wife. Me and my mates go there most days after school. I brightened up a bit. Yes, it was Chloe and Rachel, in school uniform and all wrapped up in boots and scarves, one slim and blonde, the other small and dark, heading down the bank between the rows of beeches with brown leaves still clinging on the branches. I sat up and waved like mad, but they didn't see me. Their heads were close together and they were having a good gab about something. I looked back and saw them turn into Beech Bank.

"You could be there yourself tomorrow," said Mum. "If you're not too jet-lagged."

The thought gave me a little leap of happiness inside, and made the dark grey day seem a little brighter somehow. I had missed the girls a lot, and I realised with a slightly guilty feeling that I hadn't emailed or texted as much as I could have. We'd always seemed to be on the go, out of doors most of the time and rushing from one thing to another. It would be good to catch up, and I had a lot to tell them. I'm sure they'd be fascinated by the experiences I'd had.

I don't suppose much has changed at Beech Bank though, I thought as we turned the corner and I saw our own house up ahead. Or in school, or in the town itself. It's a quiet little place, even a bit dull sometimes, and nothing much happens round here.

two

Well, I soon found I was wrong about that, for starters. If I'd thought that things back home had been dull and boring in the weeks I'd been away, I was soon brought up to speed. There'd been lots of changes.

Rachel's mum was having a baby, for a start. They already have a gazillion kids in that family, but all of them were over the moon about it. Rachel looked so smug when she told me that you'd think she was having the baby herself. Annie's mum and dad were divorcing and her dad had a new girlfriend, and you'd think she'd be gutted about that, but she seemed quite cool about it, and said she'd met the girlfriend and quite liked her.

Chloe's bossy aunt had moved in to live with them, and Chloe seemed cool about *that*. Sometimes my friends amaze me! There'd been Roma gypsy kids in school for a few weeks, and they'd made friends with a girl our age called Madalina. Madalina's uncle had given Amber a whistle that gave her power over dogs, or so she said. I've got to see that before I'll believe it!

Biggest surprise of all was Willow, who's always kind of been the leader of our group. Not only had she got rid of most of her gorgeous designer clothes and was planning a new career, but she was also in love!

Or so the other girls said. Willow denied it though.

"Can't anyone be friends with a boy without you all behaving like Year Seven giggling idiots?" she said, when they were telling me about it the first day back at school, which made them giggle a bit more, and sigh, and pull goofy love-struck faces. I noticed she went a bit pink though, which shows up on her because she has that creamy kind of skin that goes with red hair. And she was doing an awful lot of texting these days too, which was explained when I found that Jay lived in America.

In spite of all this, they wanted to hear all about my time in Australia and hung on every word I told them about the beach barbies, the awesome scenery and the Ozzie guys.

"Anyone in particular, Holls?" asked Amber innocently.

"Not really," I said. "Most of them were fit guys. We had a load of fun. But it's not all about pairing off. Being in a group is cool. There doesn't have to be anything going on if you happen to like a guy."

"That's what I've been saying," said Willow. "Thank goodness one of us at least is looking at things in a mature way."

I had to admit I was looking at things in a different way since my trip to Oz. Did that mean I was growing up? I'd always enjoyed myself, liked having a good time, being a bit flirty (or so Willow said), never had much to worry about beyond the next new outfit from Chadwick's, and generally took life for granted. I'd never even had to share with sibs, being an only child. As for my Christian life, well, my mum and dad were church people and my dad was a deacon, so that made me OK as long as I stuck to the rules, didn't it?

Or so I'd thought. I'd been a bit challenged on that in Oz. Sarah had started going to church there, and really had something going with God. They called it *relationship*, and it seemed to involve every part of their lives. Of course I knew about that from our own church, but I suddenly realised that for a lot of the time I'd been tagging along with everyone else's faith experience, my parents, the girls, our vicar and his wife. I knew I had decisions to make, whether I truly wanted God to be real in my life or not. And whether I was willing to accept the pathway he might have for me or whether I wanted to be the one making all the choices.

Anyway, I was still in the process of sorting it all out, so I didn't say much to the girls at first. I was glad to be back with them though, and to be at Beech Bank again. I'd missed it more than I'd thought.

That first afternoon back at Beech Bank stays in my mind for other reasons. Amber, Chloe and I walked part of the way home together. It got dark early now, and the shops were beginning to get their Christmas decorations and displays in the windows, and we dawdled a bit looking in. So I was a little later than usual getting home. I wasn't that late though, so I was a bit surprised to see my dad's car already parked in the drive. Dad usually got home at least an hour later than this. So I wondered what was up.

Mum and Dad were in the kitchen, sitting at the table with cooling mugs of tea in front of them. One look at their faces told me something was wrong. Badly wrong. Both of them looked up at me and smiled in a strained kind of way. My mind began to race. Something dreadful must have happened.

"Come and sit down, Holly," said Mum. "There's something we need to tell you."

My first thought was "Oh God, don't let it be Sarah!" Mum can read my mind pretty well, and she said quickly, "Don't worry, Sarah's fine, nothing to do with any of the family."

I breathed again and sat down on one of the ladder-backed chairs. Mum and Dad looked at each other, and Mum said, "I think you'd better tell her, Bob."

Tell me what, for goodness sake?

Dad cleared his throat and umm-ed and ah-ed a bit,

and then said, "Well, it's about the business. I'm afraid there are problems. Serious problems."

I breathed a sigh of relief. It was just about business. My dad runs a building firm, a very successful one, he works long hours and there are always hassles to sort out. I was quite used to that. I was getting up to get myself a juice from the fridge, but Mum said quickly, "Sit down for a minute. You need to listen."

I looked from one to the other, and Dad said, "It's very serious. The company is being handled by the receiver. We're bankrupt."

That word pulled me up short. Bankrupt? I didn't know a lot about business matters, and I realised that times were hard, not that I'm the least interested in politics or economics or anything of that kind. But bankrupt? That sounded terribly final somehow. Did it mean the end of Dad's business?

"I'm sorry," said Dad, and put his hand over his eyes. "I've let everyone down."

I looked at him in horror. I'd never seen my dad behave like this. He got up and left the room, and I heard him treading heavily up the stairs. Mum half rose to follow him, but then turned back to me. "He's terribly upset. He feels so responsible, for his own family, for his employees and their families . . ." She sat down again and put her head in her hands.

I felt stunned. I'd never seen my parents like this before. I said, "But – but – things might pick up again, mightn't they? It might just be a temporary thing."

Mum shook her head. "No. Things have been difficult for a while. We didn't want you to have to worry about it. We thought that perhaps the economy would pick up, that it was maybe just a slow spell. That's why we decided to go to Australia, while things were quiet. But it's worse now, much worse, and we just can't go on."

To my horror, she burst into tears, burying her face in her hands. I sat there feeling absolutely gobsmacked and stunned. Not by the news itself so much, but by the way my strong, capable parents had suddenly crumbled and become vulnerable and helpless. It was scary.

I wanted to comfort Mum, cheer her up, so I put my hand over hers and said the first thing that came into my head. "Mum, things will work out, you'll see. Let's plan something nice. Why don't we go into town soon. Do some Christmas shopping."

She made a strange sound, half sob, half laugh. Then she sat up straight and rubbed the tears away. "Darling, you don't understand. There'll be very little money for Christmas shopping this year. Very little for anything. Everything will have to change. This house, for instance. We're going to have to move somewhere much smaller, maybe just a flat. The cars will have to go. Thank goodness we didn't send you to that private school."

They'd really wanted me to go to a posh private school, but I'd pleaded so hard to stay with my primary school friends that I'd had my way and gone to Beechwood High.

I sat back in my chair, feeling bewildered as the truth

of the situation began to sink in. The world as I knew it seemed to be crashing down around my ears. I slowly realised there'd be no more lovely house to live in, no big shopping trips, holidays abroad. I'd taken it all for granted, but I'd enjoyed it too, enjoyed the nice clothes, riding lessons, holidays, being able to treat my friends. Maybe that visit to Sarah was the last we'd ever have. Tears filled my eyes. Big changes were ahead, and I had no idea how we were all going to cope.

three

Things seemed to be moving very fast. Within days, a For Sale sign had appeared outside our house, stuck in the front garden for everyone to see. I hated it with a force that surprised me; every time I saw the estate agent's name I felt like getting an axe and smashing the sign to pieces. It had no right to be there, sticking up among my mum's white chrysanthemums and evergreen shrubs. This was *our* house.

I felt quite sick when I realised that maybe it wouldn't be ours much longer. I almost expected a horde of people to come to the door right away wanting to buy it, tramping through the house and looking at everything. My mum would absolutely hate that and I'd hate it too.

But a day or two passed and nobody came. Mum and Dad said it was not a good time to sell property, times were hard for everyone and people were not house buying. I felt relieved; if no one bought the house then we could stay, couldn't we?

But Mum and Dad shook their heads and said no, it wasn't like that. They'd have to lower the asking price and sell the house at much less than it was worth. In any case, the bulk of the money would go towards paying the people the business owed money to. It would not be right to do otherwise, Dad said, we had obligations to fulfil. We must just get used to a much simpler way of life.

Dad looked grim most of the time, with bags under his eyes as though he didn't sleep well. Mum wasn't sleeping much either; most nights, I could hear them talking in their room far into the night, sometimes with raised voices. I heard Mum crying sometimes, too, when she thought I wasn't within earshot.

It was the smaller things that seemed to get to me most. I'd fancied a different haircut, but they told me it would cost too much. I'd thought of updating my mobile, but it was no to that too, along with a little lecture about making do with what I had. Suddenly I had to think about things like switching off lights to save electricity, making do with last year's winter jacket, things that had never entered my head before. Mum stopped shopping at the pricey supermarket and went to a cheaper cut-price one. She made most meals at home and we stopped going out to eat.

I felt really embarrassed, telling all this to the other girls at school the day after the For Sale sign went up, as though I was being disloyal to my parents or something. We were having lunch, and they all stopped eating and stared at me.

"You mean – you've lost everything?" asked Willow.

"What does that mean, exactly?" said Chloe, frowning.

"That my dad's business is bust, and our house will be sold, and our cars, and we'll hardly have enough to live on," I said, and could feel my voice beginning to shake.

"Oh no, your lovely house," said Annie.

Rachel got up and gave me a hug. Amber was looking at me with an expression I couldn't quite understand. Then she said, "In other words, you'll have to live just like the rest of us."

That gave me a shock. I hadn't thought of it like that. We'd all taken it for granted that I was the one with the expensive gear, the posh house, and everything I wanted. I'd never minded sharing with the others, and I was a bit hurt. Amber and I had always been good mates. It seemed a harsh thing to say. The others seemed to think so too.

"Oh, come on, Ams," said Willow. "That's not very nice. It must be so hard for them."

Amber went a bit pink, but she stood her ground. "Well, think about it. None of us has everything we want. It's hard for everybody. Like my mum and dad, having to work all hours 'cos they've got three kids in college as well as me and Lucy. And when you think of Madalina, and how poor her family is, and then those poor little African kids in the video we saw, with absolutely zilch, none of us should really moan about doing without nice gear and sunshine holidays, should we."

She was quite upset, and pushed her plate away across the table. I suddenly wondered whether Amber had been jealous of me all this time. I felt near to tears myself. I hadn't expected this.

The others were looking from one to the other, then Willow said, "Look, let's not quarrel about this. Holls? Ams? Let's go to Beech Bank later and talk it all over with Sadie."

But I was feeling indignant on behalf of my family now. I said, "Look, my dad worked hard to build up his business. He works long, long hours."

"And are you suggesting my dad doesn't?" demanded Amber.

I hadn't been suggesting any such thing. I'd expected support from my friends and instead somehow we were quarrelling. I felt hurt and angry and close to tears.

Willow as usual attempted to take charge and sort us out.

"Look, let's calm down. Holly, we're really sorry about what's happened – all of us. Ams, nobody's criticising your family. Don't let's fall out. We're the Beech Bank girls, remember. We stick together, no matter what the weather . . ." She got up, pushed back her chair and did a little dance to make us smile, putting on a squeaky voice and silly expression and rolling her eyes. It worked – kind of. But Amber and I didn't quite meet each other's eyes. There was a little something there between us that hadn't been there before.

Later, at Beech Bank, I got a chance to sit down and talk about my worries with Sadie. She listened, her chin in her hand and her elbows resting on the red metal table top.

"That's tough," she said, when I paused for breath. "Your poor dad. How's he taking it?"

"That's the trouble," I said, close to tears again. "Not very well. He – he seems to have shrunk somehow, and he's kind of quiet. He thinks he's let everyone down. He used to be a good laugh but I haven't seen him smile for a week. And he and Mum are arguing a lot."

I felt a tear trickle from under my eyelid and wiped it away. Sadie leaned across and took my hand. "You know what I'm going to say, don't you?"

I nodded. Pray. That's what she was going to say. And suddenly, this bitter feeling rose up inside. My mum and dad were Christians, they always prayed. I was sure they would have prayed about this too. And look where it had got them! What good was praying now? Was God going to send millions of banknotes floating down from heaven? Because that's what we'd need to get us out of this mess.

At the thought of this, I felt a wild desire to laugh, although I was crying inside. But I just nodded again, and Sadie prayed, there and then, not for money, but for God's presence with my mum and dad, and for peace in our home and guidance for the future.

Afterwards, I did feel a bit more peaceful. The other girls came over and we had coffee together.

"By the way, Holly," said Sadie, as she was getting up to go into the games room. "Have the girls told you about the different kind of Nativity play we're planning for Christmas?"

They hadn't, so they started to tell me now, all at once, butting in and interrupting each other as usual. Amber loves acting and is usually first up when there's a play or drama to be planned. But she was quieter than usual, and she wasn't quite meeting my eye.

four

It was going to be a hard winter this year, that's what everyone was saying. A sure sign had been the heavy crops of blackberries, rosehips, elderberries, nuts, and all the wild fruits in the hedgerows. And it was certainly getting colder.

My mum and dad were arguing about heating now.

"The oil tank's almost empty," said Mum, who had been out of doors early. "We need to order a refill."

"Hoped this might last out until we move," said Dad.

I was in the hallway tying my scarf for school, but even

from there I could hear the frosty pause before Mum spoke again, in jerky sentences. "That could be ages. We've got to have heat. We need to order now."

There was a small crash as though Dad had thumped the table.

"Surely we can manage. Other people do."

"Without heat, in the winter?"

"We have an Aga, for goodness sake! And an open fire! We're too mollycoddled, that's our trouble. We're owing thousands, don't forget. I'm trying to pay back all I can!"

"At the expense of your own family?"

They were really shouting now, going at it hammer and tongs. I hadn't had breakfast yet, but I decided to skip it. I couldn't bear them fighting and the horrid atmosphere I called goodbye and got out of there.

Tears blinded my eyes all the way to school, and it wasn't just because of the icy wind. My home had always been calm and peaceful. My parents hardly ever argued, and if they did, it was in a jokey kind of way. This was a whole new ball game. They sounded sometimes as though they hated each other, blamed each other for what had happened. They were going to split up, I could feel it coming and I couldn't bear it.

The other girls knew something was wrong and tried to get me to talk, but I couldn't. They might accuse me of being trivial again. Annie's parents had split up. Chloe had lost her mum and Rachel her dad. Amber had said I had to live in the real world like everyone else, hadn't she? They'd all think I was a wimp. Probably did already. Maybe they were right.

All the same, I had to talk to someone. We went to Beech Bank after school, and almost right away Sadie nabbed me and pulled me into the snug, which happened to be empty. "Holly, what on earth's wrong? You look ghastly."

And then I just burst into tears and sobbed and sobbed, with my face buried in Sadie's shoulder and tears soaking her jumper. She listened and patted me soothingly, and then said, "Well, more prayer needed, I think."

I pulled away. "We prayed before, and things have got worse."

"Yes, they often seem to. It doesn't mean God isn't listening. And can you think of anything better to do?"

I couldn't. But I still felt strangely reluctant to pray. Sadie looked at me for a moment. I felt uncomfortable and turned my head away. She was quiet for a moment, and then asked, "Holly, is there anything else bothering you?"

I didn't want to tell her about Amber and me, because it sounded kind of childish, but Sadie is the kind of person you have to be straight with. I said, "Well – Amber said something. She said, now you know what it's like for everyone else, or something like that."

"And it upset you?"

"Yes. We had a bit of a fight. It was like she was saying it served us right, that my dad didn't know what it was to work really hard like other people. And he does. It's not my fault that he's made a lot of money."

That sounded really childish. But Sadie only said, after a bit more thought, "You know, I think you ought to make up with Amber, asap. That kind of thing gets worse if it's left. Kind of festers. You and Amber are really good mates, you know."

That nearly had me blubbering again. But I was indignant too.

"It wasn't my fault! She started it!"

"All the same, maybe you should make the first move to say sorry. It's put up a barrier between the two of you, hasn't it?"

I nodded. She went on, "That kind of thing between two people creates a barrier between them and God, too. The Bible says it clearly. You need to forgive each other. And maybe it's up to you to speak first. I'll pray you have the courage to do that."

Well, I didn't think I would have the courage, prayers or not. But I knew she was right about the barrier. I could feel it, like a big heavy fence between us and a lump of misery in my stomach.

It was really cold and dark when we got out of BB. None of us wanted to hang about, even to look in the shop windows. Rachel, Annie and Willow went off one way, Chloe, Amber and I the other. Then Chloe branched off into her own street, and it was just Amber and me. Now was my chance to say something.

But I just couldn't. The big lump of misery had eased a little but now it was back, large and heavy, filling me with a kind of dread of going home, of not going home, of talking, of not talking. We walked hunched over, Amber and I, hands in pockets and faces muffled in scarves, saying nothing.

I had to break the silence, somehow. I said, "Do you think it'll snow?"

Amber grunted some kind of reply, which I couldn't hear properly and could have meant yes or no. Suddenly I could bear it no longer. We had almost reached my drive. I noticed the streetlight at the corner had a kind of halo around it from the cold. I took a deep breath and turned to Amber, opening my mouth to say, "Amber, I'm sorry I kicked off at you, I really am."

At the exact same time, she turned to me, pulled her scarf down and said, "Holls, I'm really sorry I upset you saying those things. It was mean." Then we both stopped, and both laughed, and suddenly the lump of misery just melted and was gone. We hugged each other, and both of us had tears on our cheeks, and then we laughed again, and, looking at the lights in the windows of our house, I no longer felt the same dread of what might happen to my family.

As Amber was beginning to walk away towards her own home, I felt a soft cold touch on my forehead. Amber stopped and turned back for a moment, lifting up her face to where large flakes were falling in the glow of the street light.

"Holls, look! It's snowing!"

five

It must have snowed all night, because when I looked out next morning everything was covered in a blanket of white, the shrubs in the garden, the houses beyond, even the horrid For Sale sign had its pristine covering. And it was freezing! A lot colder than usual, I thought, and when I touched the radiator I understood why, because that was cold too. I hurriedly washed and dressed and scurried down to the warm kitchen, where Mum was stirring porridge on the Aga.

"Mum, the house is freezing!"

She turned and smiled. I thought she looked a lot brighter this morning.

"Yes, I know. The heating's off. I think your dad might have a point about saving fuel, so I switched it off."

"In this weather?"

"Well, it's nice and warm in here. And we'll get the fire going in the sitting room."

I thought she must have taken leave of her senses. What a change!

"I wondered if school might be closed today," she said, putting a steaming bowl of porridge down in front of me.

I'd been wondering that too, but I hoped not, because I didn't want to spend the day cooped up in a freezing house with my mad parents. I ate my breakfast, wrapped up in coat, scarf and boots and set off. Dad must have cleared the path already from the front door to the gate. It was so cold and still out of doors, a world muffled in white. My boots were the first thing that had trodden on the snowy pavement.

I was only half-way down the hill when my phone bleeped that I had a text. It was Willow.

"School rang. Closed 2day. MayB c u l8r? My place? 11-ish, K?"

I texted back. "K. Will check with rents. C u soon."

The rents were both in the kitchen when I got back in, sitting over mugs of tea at the kitchen table. I had to say they looked more cheerful than they had lately. I told them that school was closed and that I was going to Willow's.

"Sit down and have another cup of tea first," said Mum quickly.

My heart sank. I sensed another chat coming. But I sat down and took the mug of tea she poured.

Dad cleared his throat. "We've been talking," he began. I shrank back in my seat at these ominous words. Despite their happier expressions, I had a horrid feeling I was going to hear things I didn't want to, like "separation" and "divorce" pretty soon.

"I understand better now," said Mum, and reached over to give Dad's hand a pat. "We've prayed about it and we've agreed that pulling together is the only way to get through. The house, for a start. I really think that a smaller place would be practical. And we can cut down on so many more things."

"Like heating, for instance?" It was a sarky remark, but I couldn't help it.

"Well, yes. For one thing, the kitchen's always warm, with the Aga. Thank goodness we picked an electric one. We're going to make full use of the sitting room fireplace, there are electric heaters for the bedrooms, immersion heater for the hot water. We don't need more. Such a waste heating all these rooms we don't use."

"Yes, but it's like the Arctic at the moment," I said.

"Don't be silly, dear. Your grandmothers managed perfectly well without central heating and so can we. It'll be a challenge. Your dad's going to chop up that fallen tree in the shrubbery for firewood. We have everything we need."

My mother, Mrs Perfect Housewife to Pioneer Woman! I couldn't believe it!

"Just as long as we don't get a power cut," said my dad, and both he and Mum laughed, for the first time in ages. It was a huge relief, though I still thought they'd both gone crazy.

I wished quite soon that Dad hadn't made that last remark, because not ten minutes later we did get a cut. The lights flickered out, fridge stopped humming, everything fell silent.

"Uh–oh," I said. "Power off. Now what?"

"Must be snow on the lines somewhere," said Dad. Even that didn't appear to faze him and Mum for more than a moment.

"We'll keep busy," said Dad. "Keep the blood circulating. We'll get the sitting room fire going. Then I'll make a start sawing up that tree to top up the wood supply."

"And I'll – er – do the housework," said Mum. "Wash up, make beds, vacuum . . ."

"With what?" I asked. Mum only looked nonplussed for a moment.

"Well then – broom and brush," she said. "That's what my grandmother used. You can help Dad carry in the logs."

I began to protest that I was going to Willow's, but realised that her power would be off too, so texted her, "Staying in for mo. Helping rents. MayB l8r."

All morning the sound of Dad's chainsaw echoed in the cold air. He chopped up the fallen tree and decided to cut down another couple of dead ones. My job was to split the logs into smaller chunks. Dad showed me how to do it, resting a length of log on a larger flat one, and then swinging the axe and bringing it down on the end of the topmost log. The first few times I got the axe stuck in the wood. Then I learned to let the weight of the swinging axe work for me, and heard the satisfying splintering crunch as the log split.

"Goodness knows what the Health and Safety people would say," said Dad, wiping his sweaty forehead.

"But boys and girls your age have been doing this for generations."

I soon had a gratifying barrow load of split logs to take to the house. My arms ached by lunchtime but it was a good feeling. Mum had a good fire going in the fireplace, and she heated soup in a pan over the flames. We made toast on a fork at the fire, and boiled water in another saucepan for tea.

Mum and Dad both looked slightly dishevelled and had smuts on their faces, but seemed more relaxed than they'd been for a long time. We'd just finished eating when Willow texted again. "R u coming over? Clo, Ams and mayB Rach r. Might go sledging. We r all a bit bored."

Strangely, I wasn't bored at all, and wasn't sure I wanted to go. I texted back and said I'd stay in. It was the oddest day I'd spent in a long time, but I was actually enjoying it.

Still no electricity, so no TV, computer, radio or kitchen stuff. As the short afternoon began to draw in, we lit candles and dug out some old board games we hadn't played in ages. Mum began to speculate on what we could cook for dinner on an open fire.

Dad said, gazing into the flames, "Do you remember, Beth, that camping trip in North Wales when we hadn't got two pennies to rub together? It was too cold for camping really, but we lit a big fire and huddled up in sleeping bags watching the stars come out in a frosty sky."

Mum went quite pink and gave him a soppy melting

kind of look. I should have been well embarrassed but instead I felt this kind of safe, secure feeling washing over me.

Then, suddenly, the power was back. The fridge hummed, lights flashed on, the interlude was over. Dad switched on the TV and Mum went to cook dinner in the usual way. But somehow, the peace remained.

Dad remarked, as we were watching *Shaun the Sheep* together, "Maybe I'll order that fuel. As long as we're careful with it."

I went to bed that night with a much lighter heart, clutching my hot-water bottle and pulling on my fleece bedsocks. I lay there feeling a kind of wonderment, that God answers prayer in such unexpected ways. I knew he'd answered mine, and would go on hearing and answering. I wasn't sure what the future would hold or what changes lay ahead. But I knew that, with God's help, we'd make it somehow. We'd see it through.

And I knew now that I wanted God to be the one in control of my life.

PART TWO

Amber's Story

BLIZZARD!

one

I just don't know quite what happened with me and Holly when she got back from Australia. I mean, Holls and I have been friends from our cradles, near enough. We went to the same nursery, the same primary school, high school, and of course, Beech Bank. We live practically round the corner from each other, though my house is a lot smaller and crowded and less posh than hers. And she's never had to wear her sister's hand-me-downs. Or share a bedroom and be squashed like sardines when all the family is home, like at Christmas.

I've just realised that maybe that's part of the reason we had a fall-out. Maybe I've been just a teeny-weeny bit jealous of Holly, deep down. Not that she's ever given me any reason to be, except that she's gorgeous to look at and gets her underwear in matching sets from Chadwick Teens. (Joke!) Holls always shared what she had and would give you the T-shirt off her back if you admired it.

It all seemed to come to a head when she got back from her fabulous trip to Oz.

There were the rest of us, putting up with the grey, miserable November weather, sniffling with head colds and wrestling with the end-of-term exams. And here comes Holls, with a deep golden tan and sun-bleached streaks in her hair, bringing pressies all round and telling us about the amazing time she'd had surfing, snorkelling, sightseeing, soaking up the sun and so on and so on. It made our lives here seem very plain and dull.

And then what happens? Next day, she's in floods of tears, because her dad's business is in trouble, they have to move, they have no money, it's the end of the world, blah blah blah.

Well. The other girls were all sympathy and hugs, but suddenly I had this feeling – well, Holls, welcome to the real world! It's what we all have to put up with, day in day out. And I said it. Just like that. Mostly it's Rachel who does this, but this time it was me. The words came out before I could stop them. And I regretted it the moment I'd spoken.

I know I'm supposed to be a drama queen, but I'd never had such an effect before with something I said. The other girls all stared at me as though I'd pulled a knife on someone. Holly looked as though I'd stabbed her in the back, and Willow said, "Oh, come on, Ams. That's not very nice."

If I'd had any sense at all I would have said sorry, there and then, and that would have been an end to it. But instead I heard myself blathering away about poor people and the hardship in the world, all the time digging myself in deeper and deeper. Holly looked close to tears, but then she flared up at me and accused me of criticising her family. Everything was kicking off, getting out of control, just because of those few words I said. Willow stepped in and tried to cool it down by making us laugh. But I knew Holly hadn't forgotten and neither had I. And I was miserable, because I'd started it.

Anyway, on the surface we carried on as normal. At Beech Bank I saw Holly go off to have a chat with Sadie. I'd have liked to talk myself, but couldn't quite bring myself to do it. I was a bit ashamed, to tell the truth. And then later they were all talking about the Christmas play.

A few days later Mum reminded me that I had to move my stuff to get ready for Christmas. Not only would I have to share with my big sister Kim, but we'd also have to have Lucy in the room with us as well, sleeping on a little camp bed, because both my brothers were coming home too.

"You'll need to pack away all that stuff on the floor to make room for Lucy's bed," said Mum, pointing to the piled-up bags, books and bits of clothing.

I added my school bag to the rest. "Do I have to?"

"Yes, you do. Put everything away in the drawers and cupboards. There's plenty of room if you'd keep things tidy." She gave me a keen look. "And cheer up. You've been looking a bit grumpy lately."

I started to pick up my stuff, chucking shoes and clothes into the wardrobe and piling books on the desk. A few layers down I discovered my Bible, and realised I hadn't opened it for days. Sadie and Rod always tell us the

Bible is like spiritual food; we need it every single day like our actual food, if we're to stay healthy. Somehow these last few days I hadn't bothered. Or maybe didn't want to be bothered.

I picked it up and flicked over a few pages, reading a few words or a sentence here and there. Then suddenly I stopped turning pages and looked properly. People talk about verses seeming to jump off the page, and that was happening now. They were in the epistle of James, and were about the tongue and the words we speak.

* * *

A word out of your mouth may seem of no account, but it can accomplish nearly anything – or destroy it. It only takes a spark, remember, to set off a forest fire!

* * *

I sat down on the bed, still holding the Bible. I'd forgotten just who James was, the one who wrote that book of the Bible, but I knew exactly what he was talking about. A few words from me had caused a lot of pain and grief, and I had to do something about it.

I got the chance next day, when Holly and I were walking home from Beech Bank together. It was freezing cold. I wasn't finding it easy to speak, but I knew I had to do it. We got to her house and I knew it was now or never. I took a deep breath, sent up a quick prayer, turned to her and said, "Holls, I'm so sorry I said those things. It was mean."

And would you believe it, she was starting to apologise to me! She said she'd been miserable too! But suddenly it was all OK again. I breathed another little prayer, of thanks this time. God is so good! And as though to put the icing on the cake, it was snowing! I just love snow!

Next morning, I couldn't wait to get outside into the winter wonderland that had appeared overnight. I let our dog, Hamlet, out in the garden for a run before breakfast and he loved the snow too. He stuck his nose into it and woofed in surprise at the coldness, and then raced round and round in circles kicking up white flurries. I went inside, laughing, to get ready for school.

"Well, it's nice to see you looking cheery again," said Mum. "Don't forget to call in at the surgery on your way home from school for your tetanus injection."

That took the smile off my face. I'd forgotten the dreaded tetanus jab. I hate, hate, hate injections!

"Oh, Mum! Do I have to?"

"Yes, you do. Four-fifteen."

"Maybe it'll be cancelled. Maybe the surgery will be closed because of the snow."

"It won't. Don't make such a fuss! It'll all be over in a second."

"But I hate needles!"

"It's nothing. Honestly, Lucy makes less fuss than you do! Do you want me to come with you?"

I didn't. My street cred would suffer badly if my mum had to take me to the doctor's like a little kid. I said,

"No thanks. I'll manage. But don't blame me if you get a phone call saying I've fainted. Don't say I didn't warn you."

"You won't faint," said Mum, in a voice that meant there was to be absolutely no more discussion on the subject.

two

I hadn't even left the house when the phone rang with the message that our school was closed. Also, the primary school was closed too, which meant no school for Lucy and no work for Mum, who's a dinner lady at Lucy's school. The three of us stood in the kitchen, all more or less wrapped up to face the elements, and looked at each other.

"Well," said Mum, beginning to unpeel her long scarf. "That's us with a free morning then. What shall we do? Have a girls' baking session? You used to love those, Amber."

"When I was about her age," I said, looking at Lucy, who had plonked down on the floor and begun to pull off her red spotty wellie boots.

Mum ignored that. "A nice big batch of mince pies would be good," she said. "Some for now, some to freeze ready for Christmas. Do you want to cut out the pastry, Lucy?"

Lucy did. I sighed. Making mince pies was not my idea of a fun morning. I texted Chloe and Willow to see what they were doing, which was nothing much, so we agreed to text the others and all meet up at Willow's.

And then the power went off, and that plan was abandoned.

"Thank goodness for a gas cooker," said Mum. "Let's get on with the baking."

So mince pies it was. It was quite good fun actually. I'd forgotten how much I used to enjoy rolling pastry, and how delicious was the smell of pies baking. All of us got rather floury and sticky, and Hamlet gobbled a big lump of uncooked pastry that Lucy dropped on the floor, but we kept warm and enjoyed ourselves.

Willow texted soon after lunch and said they were going sledging on the steep field out by Rachel's house, and had I got a sledge I could bring? I went out to rummage for our red plastic one from last year and found it under some other stuff in the shed. Lucy begged to come too, but Mum distracted her by promising to help her build a snowman. "You can take Hamlet though," she said. "He's looking a bit iffy after that uncooked pastry. If he's going to throw up, I'd rather he did it outside than in."

Hamlet was keen to go, and forgot any notions of throwing up once he was out of doors. He has a cast iron stomach, that dog. When he was younger he once ate a rubber spider, a dead bird, and one and a half socks of

my dad's, all in the same day, and never turned a hair.
On the other hand, he was violently sick after getting
into a box of chocolates. My big bro Charlie is training to
be a vet and said it was a good thing, because chocolates
are poisonous for dogs.

Anyway, Hamlet would have liked to run riot in the
snow, but I kept him on the lead, which was quite
complicated as I was towing the sledge as well. It was
kind of exhilarating being out in the snow, with the cold
air biting at my cheeks and a covering of white on every
twig and branch. Even the dustbins had a little extra
lid of snow on top. I passed Holly's house and could
hear a chainsaw working round the back. Holls had
said she was helping her mum and dad, and as I went
by, the chainsaw paused and I heard the sound of her
and her dad laughing together. Things must be better
with them, I thought. I'd have stopped by to say hello,
but Hamlet was tugging at the lead and looking like he
might get tangled up with the sledge ropes so I didn't
stop. Charlie says he needs obedience training and I
think he's right.

Chloe and Annie were already at Willow's, and Chloe
had brought her sledge along, same as mine but green.
Rachel met us at the end of her road, and we turned
into the big sloping field that was some kind of common
ground. At any rate, loads of kids from town always came
out to sledge and toboggan here whenever there was
snow. There were lots of people there already, families
pulling toddlers on little sledges, older kids, a group of

boys from our school having a snowball fight. We were half tempted to join in.

"Those guys think they're the business," said Rachel. "I bet we could easily make them squeal."

I could see she was itching to get in on the action. The others were less keen.

"Then we'd have to spend the rest of the day with snow down our necks and in our boots and everywhere," said Annie. "Yuck!"

"Yeah, let's sledge first and then give them a battering on the way home," said Chloe. That sounded like a good idea.

"It's crowded here, though," said Willow, looking at the small bodies hurtling down and usually falling off, and mums rushing to pick up capsized and yelling infants.

"We could go on to the next field," said Rachel. "There's a stile in the hedge along here somewhere."

"But doesn't that field belong to someone?" asked Willow.

Rachel shrugged. "It belongs to the farm, I think. But there's a footpath that goes through. And I know the farmer, he's got horses and we go round to have a ride sometimes. It'll be OK."

We traipsed across the slope, away from the sledgers and snowballers, although one of the boys fired a parting shot that hit Chloe on the shoulder. Rachel looked round. "Ben Freeman. We'll get him on the way back. He fancies you, Clo."

"Yeah yeah," said Chloe, brushing snow from her jacket. The snow was deep here and all of us were glad we'd put on wellies and not worn our Uggs. We found the stile in the hedge and hauled ourselves, Hamlet and the sledges over into the next field.

We were round the other side of the hill now, and the voices and shrieks of the other people faded into the distance. We were in a long, snow-covered field, empty except for a small stone building almost at the top of the slope. The expanse of pure whiteness stretched away into the distance. We plodded up the slope, towing our sledges.

"This is where the horses are usually," said Rachel. "All nice and warm in their stables now."

"Should be a good run down," I said, panting a little.

Chloe was looking speculatively at Hamlet, who was frisking around in the snow now I'd let him off the lead.

"I've just been reading this book, *The Call of the Wild*," she said. "I'm wondering if we could use Hamlet as a sled dog."

The others thought this was hilarious, and had a good laugh, which I personally took as insulting. They're always picking on poor Hamlet, although, if I was honest, I didn't hold out much hope for success in getting him to mush on command. Or do much else on command.

"Maybe not," I said.

We were all well warmed up from walking uphill with the sledges, and thought we'd reached a good starting point, a flatter space at the top of a rise. The snow was powdery and good to go. Willow and Rachel went first, starting slowly and working up to a good speed by the time the ground levelled out again. Chloe and me next. Then Annie and Willow. Then Rach and Chloe. Then me and Annie. And so on. Hamlet pranced beside us every time we pushed off, barking his head off. The feel of cold air rushing past our faces was exhilarating. We were warm as toast from pulling the sledges uphill. We were having the best time.

three

We were having the best time, that is, until disaster struck. After a while, it got a bit boring waiting to take turns on the sledge. Someone suggested doubling up, two at a time, then only one would be left waiting for their turn. The sledges were only meant for one, but we found we could squeeze on two at a time, though with arms and legs sticking out at all angles, and it was a bit perilous on the corners if we tried to steer. Still, it was OK, and a good giggle.

I was the odd one waiting at the top of the run when it happened. Even Hamlet had deserted me, insisting on running with the sledges every time they pushed off, barking all the way. I could hear a lot of shrieks and giggles. Then, suddenly, a piercing scream.

One of the sledges – the green one – had capsized almost at the bottom of the slope, and one of the girls – Annie – was huddled in the snow, clutching her leg and sobbing. I ran down to join them, floundering through powdery snow. "What happened?"

Willow had her arm round Annie, helping her sit up. I pushed away Hamlet, who was trying to lick Annie's face.

"The sledge tipped," said Chloe. "Hit a bump or something."

Annie was sitting in the snow, white and shaky but trying to smile. "My own stupid fault. I was trying to turn the sledge and got my leg stuck underneath. Twisted my ankle."

"Maybe riding two up wasn't such a good idea," said Willow. "Anyway, let's go back up to the hut and have a look at it."

"We can tow you on the sledge," said Rachel.

Between us, we hoisted Annie onto the green sledge and pulled her to the top of the rise. Annie's a slim girl, but even so it was hard work. We were all puffing when we got there. We pulled the sledge right inside the hut, where it was dim and musty, half-full of hay bales, obviously a store for winter fodder.

Willow sat Annie on a bale and carefully pulled off her wellie and then her thick sock. The ankle was already beginning to look bruised and puffy, but Annie could wiggle her toes so nothing seemed to be broken.

She thought she could stand, but when she tried, sat down again very quickly with tears in her eyes. "It really hurts!"

"A sprain," said Willow. "They're really painful. We need to bind it up to stop it swelling. What can we use?"

"A scarf?" said Rachel. "Here, take mine."

Most of us had long woolly scarves, but Rachel's was made of firmer woven material. Willow wound it round Annie's ankle and tucked in the ends.

"That feels better," said Annie. "Thanks."

Willow pulled on Annie's sock over the makeshift bandage, but it was impossible to put on her wellie.

"We'll have to tow you home," said Rachel. "Or maybe to my place, it's the closest. Better start right away. It's getting dark."

In the short while we'd been in the hut, the daylight had suddenly faded, and it wasn't just because of the dim interior. When Chloe and I went to the door, we could see that it was snowing again. Not just a gentle fall either. This was a real snowstorm, a whirling mass of flakes in a darkening sky. A blizzard had blown up.

Chloe and I went back to report to the others, sitting on either side of Annie on the hay bales.

"I think we'd better phone and ask someone to come and get us," said Willow.

We debated who to phone. Most of the dads would not be home from work yet.

"Mine will though," said Chloe. "He's working from home today."

She dialled the number. Nothing happened. "It's flat," she said. "Lend me yours, Ams."

But the result was the same. "They can't all be flat," said Willow, when we'd tried the others too. She paused ominously before she went on, "You know what it is? There's no signal. We're in a kind of blind spot here, this side of the hill."

We looked at the non-existent signal on our phones, then at each other in the gloom. We'd been warm from the exercise but now a cold chill was creeping into the building. It was getting darker. Night was coming, and one of us was injured.

"They'll come looking for us, I expect," said Willow bracingly.

"'Course they will," said Rachel. "And if they don't know where we are, they'll be able to follow our tracks in the snow."

This thought cheered us for a while, until Rachel and I went to the doorway again. In the light that was left, we could just see that the tracks we'd made were rapidly filling up with fresh snow. And it was still snowing. We looked at each other. Soon there'd be no trace of us.

We sat on the straw bales, and tried to think positive. Annie was close to tears, though she said it was because her foot was hurting. None of us had brought bags or rucksacks, so we had no food or drink. We searched our pockets, and Rachel found two painkillers, which she gave to Annie. Chloe had half a bag of crisps and I had a tube of Rolos, which we shared between us. Willow had a bottle of water, but it only had a small amount left in it, which she gave to Annie to wash down the tablets. The Rolos gave us a small sugar rush that made us feel a bit better.

"This reminds me of a book I read," said Chloe. "It was called *Ethan Frome*. He was a farmer with an invalid wife. He hired a girl to look after his wife, then he and the girl fell in love. The wife sent her packing, and made the husband take the girl to the train station. Instead, they spent the whole afternoon tobogganing down a steep hill, until they crashed into a tree and were nearly killed. They ended up seriously disabled, with the invalid wife looking after them both."

"That makes me feel a lot better, not," said Rachel. "Now I wonder, if Hamlet was a different kind of dog, we could maybe tie a note to his collar and send him home for help."

I didn't think it likely that Hamlet would oblige.

"But we must do *something*," said Chloe. "We can't just sit here all night."

"Maybe two of us could go for help and the other two stay with Annie," said Willow.

That sounded like the best idea yet. "Who goes and who stays?" said Rachel. "I'll volunteer to go, for one."

"I'll go too, if you like," I said, although I had a sudden mental image of Captain Oates going off into the South Pole blizzard and saying he might be gone some time.

But when we went to the door again, Rachel stopped

dead. It was almost pitch dark now, and the snow was still coming thick and fast. "Ams," said Rachel. "I don't know which way to go. Can you remember?"

I couldn't. The blizzard was blocking out any lights that might have shown from town, or maybe the power was still off. I tried to remember in which direction the doorway of the hut had been facing, and completely failed. Rachel knew her house was just across a field or two, but couldn't for the life of her work out which way it might be.

We closed the heavy door and went slowly back to the others huddled in the hay bales, their shapes just visible. In spite of everything, I couldn't resist squeezing the last bit of drama out of the situation.

"Girls," I said. "We can't find the way. There's no escape. We're trapped."

four

I couldn't see their faces, but I heard a gasp and sensed them all tensing up.

"What do you mean, trapped?" asked Annie in a quavery voice.

"We can't remember the direction," I said, fumbling about for a bale to sit on. Hamlet was pressing up against me and whining. He wanted to go home too.

"We could just blunder about in circles and get nowhere," said Rachel.

"Until we fell exhausted in the snow," I added.

I wondered if they'd think Rachel and I were just being wimpy, but then Chloe said, "Yes, that could easily happen. Remember in one of the *Little House on the Prairie* books, there was a blizzard and someone walked within feet past a cabin and headed out into the open prairie."

"No point in taking risks," said Willow. "We'll just have to sit it out."

"You mean – all night?"

"Maybe. If someone doesn't find us."

"But it's so cold. Won't we freeze to death?"

"How long does it take to die of hydrophobia?"

"You mean hypothermia. I don't know. I think if you stay awake it's all right."

"We mustn't go to sleep then. We'll have to keep each other awake."

"I wish we had some food."

"We won't die of starvation in one night. It takes about three weeks."

"We haven't got water either. How long can you last without water?"

We were working ourselves up into a right old panic now. Another few minutes and we'd be getting hysterical. Willow took charge, as usual.

"Look, we should be able to last out a few hours until

morning. As soon as it's daylight, some of us can go for help. We just have to keep warm."

We were already shivering, partly from cold but also with nervous tension. Then Rachel remembered something.

"I think hay will keep you warm if you burrow into it. It can be used as insulation. I heard somewhere that people even used to use hay for cooking, in something called a hay box."

"But this is all baled up," said Chloe. "We'd need it loose. Would the farmer mind if we took the bales to pieces?"

"I think he'd rather find loose hay than five bodies," said Rachel, which made Annie give a little shriek. Willow said, "Oh, shut up, Rach. Let's get some bales untied."

Chloe discovered a little pair of folding nail scissors in a jacket pocket, and we used this to cut the string holding the bales. We loosened two or three and made a kind of nest among the other bales. We blundered about a bit in the near-darkness, bumping into one another, but the activity warmed us up a little and made us feel we were doing something useful. Rachel discovered some thick folded blankets on a manger at one end of the building, which she said by the smell of them, must belong to the horses. "We can use them as extra covers," she said.

For some reason, the discovery of the horse blankets cheered us up no end. We burrowed into the hay and arranged the blankets over and around us. Hamlet pushed in amongst us too, bewildered at our strange behaviour but not wanting to miss out on anything.

"I feel warmer already," said Rachel, but she sounded as though she was half trying to convince herself as much as anything. Still, it did seem to be warmer, huddled together in a mass of prickly hay and horsy-smelling blanket. The hay was itchy though.

"Do horses get fleas?" asked Annie suddenly, which made us all jump and start scratching the itchy places.

"No, they don't," said Willow firmly, though I had the feeling she was only saying that to ward off another attack of panic.

"How's your ankle, Annie?" asked Rachel.

"Better, thanks, since I took the painkillers. Still throbbing a bit though."

"Keep it up as much as possible. Stick it up on that bale in front."

There was more shuffling and rustling as Annie arranged herself. People's knees and elbows seemed to be everywhere, and Hamlet didn't help by trying to turn round and round, as dogs do. It was going to be an uncomfortable night.

"Remember, don't go to sleep," said Chloe warningly.

Being overtaken by sleep seemed to me the least of our worries, in the circumstances.

"I'm so hungry," said Rachel. "We were having steak and kidney pie for tea this evening. With peas and mash."

"We were having beef casserole," said Chloe. "Auntie Sue was getting it ready when I came out. And syrup pudding after."

I thought longingly of the mince pies we'd made that very morning. And fish and chips. And Chinese takeaway. And eggs and bacon. Bangers and mash. Chilli with rice. Lasagne with cheese topping.

Food was on all of our minds.

"I read this book once," said Chloe. We all groaned. But she went on, "It was a bit gruesome, but it was true. This group of pioneers were crossing the Sierra Nevada mountains and got cut off by snow. They were there all winter. They ate all the food, then they ate the horses and cattle, then they cut the harness into little bits and ate that. Then – they started eating each other."

"What? You're just making that up!"

"No, it's true. People died and they ate the bodies. Or bits of them."

"Do you think we might come to that?" said Annie faintly.

"No, of course not. I was just saying."

"I must say, Chloe, you read some very depressing books," said Willow. "Haven't you read anything about people surviving blizzards and coming through unscathed?"

Chloe thought for a moment. "I don't know about unscathed. Mostly, they get frostbite and have to chop off their fingers and toes."

That got us all checking our own fingers and toes. They were cold, but frostbite had not set in yet, we decided. Chloe thought for a little longer. "I did read this story called *The Post Horn*, about a Swiss postman who fell into a drift and survived for days, then dug himself out with his post horn and staggered on to deliver the mail."

"I wish we had a post horn," said Rachel gloomily. "Or a hunting horn, or a vuvuzela horn, or even a police whistle. If we could just let people know where we are."

We shuffled about some more, trying to get comfortable and not succeeding very well.

And then Willow suddenly shot upright and gave me a fright. A sudden horrible thought came into my mind. "Willow – do you think there are mice in here? Or even *rats*?"

This brought a chorus of shrieks. My brother Sam had been teaching Hamlet the word "rats" last time he was home, and Hamlet leapt up and began barking into the darkness.

"For goodness sake!" said Willow. "If there are any, they'll keep a very low profile with us lot around! I just thought of something. We're such numpties! We should have thought of it ages ago."

five

There was an expectant hush; although we couldn't see each other I knew our heads had all turned towards Willow.

"We haven't prayed," she said. "We've thought of all those other things to do, and we didn't even think of praying. I can't believe it!"

We were all silent for a moment. It was true. We had pondered and planned and schemed, and nothing we'd thought of had come to anything. I felt rather ashamed, and wondered if this happens a lot, that people in trouble do everything they can think of to get out of it by themselves and only turn to God when there's nothing else left.

Willow seemed to have been thinking along the same lines. She said, "Thank goodness God doesn't hold it against us when we try to do things our way."

Annie said tremulously, "I was thinking about praying, but then I thought that maybe God wouldn't listen, as it's all my fault really we're in this mess. If I hadn't tried to be clever and show off on the sledge . . ."

We all tried to reassure her.

"It wasn't your fault, Annie."

"Could have been any of us."

"Nobody's blaming you."

"Anyway," said Willow. "God isn't like that. If we've made stupid mistakes, or even gone right against him on purpose, he's always glad when we come back to him. Think about the story of the Prodigal Son. The father was so pleased to see him that he ran down the road to meet him when he was just a little speck in the distance. That's what God is like."

All of us seemed to be suddenly more cheerful. You

could feel it, even though we couldn't see each other's faces.

"Well, let's pray then," said Rachel.

So we did, holding hands in the darkness amongst the scratchy hay, with the snow whipping against the outside of the building. One by one we told God how scared we were, deep down, and asked him to help us get home safe.

We were quiet for a while after that. Even Hamlet seemed to settle down, in fact he fell asleep and began to snore. The sound was strangely comforting. Chloe gave a sigh. "It's quite a relief, isn't it, to think that it's up to God now, what happens."

The rest of us agreed. The prayers had calmed us and stopped the panicky thoughts and fears that had been arising.

"God won't let us die," said Annie, voicing what I'd been thinking.

"Mind you," said Chloe thoughtfully, "Everyone does, sooner or later. Even young people sometimes."

I sensed a change in the general mood again, and I was going to say something sarky to Chloe about reading too many books, when I suddenly remembered that her brother Peter has a serious condition that means he could potentially die at any time. So I shut up. Chloe is the kindest person I know, and wasn't trying to scare us. She was just stating a fact.

"The thing to remember," said Willow, "is that God has already decided how long we should live, even before we were born. Remember that verse, I think it's in Psalm 139, '*All the days ordained for me were written in your book before one of them came to be.*'"

Remembering that verse just took my breath away. To think that God has my lifespan all planned out like that.

"That's so awesome," said Rachel. "I read it when Mum told us she's having another baby."

"Know what?" said Annie suddenly. "I feel like singing! Let's sing a song! How about that one Chloe wrote for Rod's Beech Bank competition, 'Sing for Joy'?"

The idea of singing for joy seemed a bit strange, given the situation we were in, but Annie started it up and we all joined in, a bit quavery at first:

* * *

Sing for joy, all you lands
Praise the Lord and clap your hands.
How awesome is our God most high
Maker of earth and heaven and sky.
Trumpets sound and voices raise,
Sing to him a psalm of praise.
Glorious in his majesty,
Every king shall bend the knee.

* * *

By the time we got to the chorus, "*Sing praises to our God, Sing praises to our King,*" we really were singing from our hearts and feeling a whole lot better. Warmer, too; the cold feel of anxiety had lifted from us all, and not just on the outside. We sang it through again and then again. Hamlet was puzzled but then decided he'd join in and gave a heart-rending howl, which made us all laugh.

We were just getting our breaths back when Hamlet suddenly stiffened and then leapt out from amongst us and stood over by the door, barking furiously. We all shot up and most of us scrambled to our feet, shedding hay in all directions. Rachel opened the door. It was still snowing heavily, but there was a sound in the stillness, a definite sound of an engine, and I thought for a moment I saw a gleam of light in the darkness. We stood shivering in the doorway and listened.

"It's a tractor!" said Rachel. "It's coming across the field! Look, there are the headlights!"

It was a tractor, and it was heading in our very direction.

"Wave!" said Willow. "Wave so they'll see us!"

We waved and shouted, but we needn't have worried, because the tractor was clearly heading for our barn. It ploughed up through the snow and stopped, and we heard men's voices calling our names.

"Dad!" shrieked Chloe, and then I heard the sound of my own dad's voice, and I've never heard anything so wonderful in my life. My dad was there, and Chloe's, and Willow's, and Rachel's stepdad, plus the farmer and a couple of other men. There was a lot of hugging and questions and a few tears, then one of them picked up Annie and herded the rest of us and Hamlet out through the blizzard to the tractor, and piled us in, some in the cab and others in the box behind. The farmer never said a word about the mess in his barn, in fact he seemed overjoyed that we'd taken shelter there. We had a short bumpy ride across fields and through gateways until we ended up at Rachel's house, being the nearest of our homes, where we quickly piled out and went inside.

I'd never seen anything so welcoming as Rachel's living room, with the woodburner blazing, lights on, and comfy chairs and sofas. We girls looked a sorry sight, bedraggled and shivering, with bits of hay sticking to our clothes and hair. Rachel's mum gave us all hot chocolate, checked Annie's ankle, which she thought was a sprain but not a bad one, and decided that the rest of us were a bit cold but nothing serious.

A lot of phoning was going on, letting families know we'd been found. We began to feel apologetic at the trouble we'd caused.

"We're so sorry to get you out so late," said Willow.

"Late?" said Chloe's dad. "It's only just six o'clock, you know."

Sure enough, the TV was on and we could see the six o'clock news was just beginning. It had seemed like half the night, but we'd actually only been missing for an hour or so.

"How did you know where to look for us?" asked Rachel curiously.

"It was that boy, Ben Freeman," said Ted, her stepfather. "When none of you turned up home for tea, we started asking around among the people who'd been out sledging. That boy remembered seeing you go off across the field and climb the stile. Thank goodness he noticed!"

"I told you he fancied you, Clo," said Rachel.

I expected my parents to really kick off for giving them such a scare. They were quite good about it, though. I think everyone was relieved to get us back in one piece, more or less, with never a hint of frostbite or hypothermia or starvation. I breathed a prayer of thankfulness when I went to bed that night. Mum came to tuck me in, which she hadn't done since I was pretty much Lucy's age.

"I know you're a bit of a drama queen, Amber," she said, with a twinkle in her eye. "But don't you think getting stranded in a remote hut in a blizzard is a bit extreme just to get out of a tetanus jab?"

The dreaded doctor's appointment had completely slipped my mind.

"Does that mean I can forget about it now?" I asked hopefully.

"No chance," said Mum.

PART THREE

Chloe's Story

BABYSITTING BLUES

one

The first thing I wanted to do after the sledging adventure was write a story about it. I was thinking over titles even before we got home that evening, when we were drinking hot chocolate and warming up at Rachel's. "In the teeth of the blizzard" was one. Or "Stranded – how we survived a night in Arctic conditions". Although Rachel quickly pointed out that I couldn't have such a misleading title, as we'd only been stranded for about an hour. All the same, our rescue had been an exciting event, with snowflakes whirling in the tractor's headlights, and the dark shapes of big men jumping down to save us.

Auntie Sue, who looks after us at home, is a bit of a worrier and had apparently been quite frantic when I failed to turn up for tea, according to my brother Peter. When I got home she insisted on putting me to bed immediately, although it was only 8.30 and I wanted to watch TV. She filled two hot-water bottles and put an extra blanket over my duvet, although by then I was warm as toast. Hungry though. Auntie Sue, bless her, brought my supper up on a tray and probably would have fed me with a spoon if I'd complained of weakness and tiredness. I spotted

Peter grinning at me from the doorway and pulled a face at him. I must have been tired though, because I fell asleep almost as soon as I'd finished.

In the morning, the snow had stopped falling, though it was now several inches deeper than it had been the day before. The snowploughs had been out overnight, school was open again and life seemed to be going on as usual, except that there was a backdrop of pristine white fields and hills all round the town, and a covering of snow on the rooftops and every other surface.

All of us were at school except Annie, who had seen the doctor to get her ankle strapped up and been told to keep it up for a few days. They said we'd done the right thing binding it up to minimise swelling, and they'd given Annie some crutches.

We weren't sure Beech Bank would be open after school, but saw that the lights were on there and it was business as usual. Sadie was there, and seemed a bit preoccupied, with a little worried frown on her forehead. "I'm so glad to see you girls! We heard about your little adventure! Are you all OK, except for Annie?"

News travels fast in a small town. We told her we were fine. She went on, "I hate to ask so soon afterwards, but I'm really desperate for a babysitter tomorrow evening. Christmas will be here before we know it, and we've got to crack on with our Nativity play preparations if we're going to be ready in time. The council committee have agreed to see me tomorrow evening about the street lighting and so on. Rod has another meeting that night and there's no granny available then either."

"No probs," said Willow. "We'll sort something out between us, won't we, girls?"

We agreed. We'd done it often enough before.

I should mention that Sadie is not your ordinary run-of-the-mill vicar's wife. Maybe there's no such thing, but I'd always imagined them to be middle-aged ladies in twin-sets and pearls, arranging flowers in the church and graciously presiding at tea parties with other ladies. Sadie's clothes mostly come from charity shops or boot sales, though she knows how to put things together to look mega-cool.

We'd been babysitting, Willow and Amber and I, when Sadie first told us about her earlier life, and that also was not what you'd have expected for a future vicar's wife. She'd come home early that night; she and Rod had both had separate meetings to go to and for some reason hers had been cancelled at the last minute. It was summer, and instead of going home right away, Sadie suggested we sat out on the patio for a bit with juice and nibbles. It was peaceful there, with the kids asleep and the sun making long shadows on the vicarage lawn. Sadie kicked off her sandals and stretched out her long legs, leaning back in her deckchair.

"It's a relief to get out of that meeting! Who'd have ever thought it? That I'd be on the church ladies flower-arranging rota?"

She giggled a bit.

"What *did* you think you'd be?" asked Willow, who

was planning a career in fashion design at the time, though she's had other ideas since.

Sadie thought for a while before replying. "I didn't think ahead much when I was your age. In fact, I was a bit of a mess all round."

We pricked up our ears. Sadie was serious now. "I'm so glad you girls have more sense than I had."

We looked at each other. "That's not what my dad says," said Amber, and I could see she'd have said more, but we all noticed that Sadie was looking really serious now and not joking.

"What happened?" asked Willow.

"I guess I rebelled, big time," said Sadie slowly. "My parents were strict, very strict and I was an only child. Lots of rules. They expected a lot of me." She paused for a moment, her face sad. "Well, I wouldn't have it. I hated rules. Still not keen for that matter."

"What did you do?" asked Amber. We were all holding our breaths now.

"Everything I could that they'd hate. Got into bad relationships. Ran away from home a couple of times. Got into drugs."

I couldn't hold back a gasp. "Sadie, you didn't do drugs?"

She nodded. "Fortunately no long-term damage, thank God. And I really mean that, because it was God who got me out of it. In the shape of some people who were out in town most nights looking out for young people who might be in trouble. They really showed me what love was all about, and even got me to see that my parents had only made the rules because they loved me. Maybe they came down too hard, but it was because they cared."

We were all quiet for a moment, and then Amber said what we were all thinking. "Don't you – don't you find it hard to be a vicar's wife, and kind of have to set an example, when you know you did all those things?"

Sadie looked at her and smiled, pushing back her unruly dark hair. "No. And you know why? Because when we come to Jesus and say we're truly sorry, he gives us a brand new start. Everything we've ever done is forgiven and forgotten. It's like we're being given a second chance. Maybe that's why they call it being born again."

Her smile was so radiant that we knew it had happened for her exactly as she said. God had changed that messed-up, rebellious teenager into the confident, capable, gorgeous young woman Sadie is today. I was glad she'd told us. It didn't change our opinion of her one little bit. In fact, since that summer evening we've admired and respected and looked up to her even more.

So we're always glad when we can do something to help her. Even when it's babysitting Josh and Abi, who are cute as can be and are often sweet and adorable, though I have to say they can also be noisy, messy, obstreperous and a lot of hard work.

two

In the end, it was me, Willow and Amber who volunteered for babysitting duty. Annie was out of it because of her injury, Rachel lives a bit too far out on the edge of town to make it safe or wise for her to get to the Vicarage in the evening, after dark, with snow on the ground and slippery pavements. As for Holly, she's spending so much time with her parents these days that you'd think they were all joined at the hip.

So it was the three of us turning up at the Vicarage after we'd had our tea, and stamping the snow off our boots on the porch.

Rod was out at some parish council meeting it seemed, and Sadie was all excited about seeing the town council. It was quite important apparently. Sadie had got this idea about a new-style Nativity play back in the late summer, when Christmas seemed far in the future. It seemed she'd seen an account of the way another small town had done it, and thought it would be brilliant for us. She told us about it over coffee one afternoon at Beech Bank.

"The usual type of Nativity plays can get a bit boring, don't you think?"

We couldn't help agreeing. All of us had seen the usual efforts, and taken part in them ourselves. Little kids in dressing-gowns and tea-towels on their heads, a pretty little girl in blue as Mary, clutching a doll and sometimes dropping it, other kids dressed up as sheep or camels, or kings, or donkeys, forgetting their lines and fidgeting and scratching themselves because the costumes were itchy. I'd been an angel once, and Molly Mills, who was also an angel, was jealous because I had bigger wings than hers. She pulled my hair when we were waiting off-stage to "appear" to the shepherds. I pulled hers back, a fight broke out in the angel ranks, and by the time we arrived on stage we all had haloes askew, wings dropping and murderous expressions on our faces. I smiled at the memory.

"What we need," said Sadie, "is to get to the heart of the Christmas story, convey the reality and the human side of it. Get across what it must have meant for them all. For Joseph, finding that his fiancé was pregnant, presumably having been unfaithful to him. And Mary herself. What a scary, awesome thing to be happening to a young girl. She was probably not much more than your ages, you know."

That made us all stop and think. A teenager our age, being told she was going to give birth to someone who would be the Saviour of the world! What an awesome responsibility.

"Do you think she had a choice in it?" asked Holly.

"I think she did," said Sadie. "Remember, she agreed to whatever God wanted. She was so brave. Unmarried mothers were despised in those days and that culture. She'd have been shunned by her society. Maybe even stoned, when the news got out."

"She wouldn't have been given counselling and put on benefits and given a council flat," said Amber, which made us all smile but brought a serious note to the conversation too.

"No, she'd have depended on her family to support her," said Sadie. "And Joseph. He was such a man of faith too, deciding to take care of her when he probably didn't fully understand what was happening. That's what I want to depict in our play. The human side, as well as the wonder of God's plan."

We were getting interested now. This wasn't going to be just another run-of-the-mill Christmas show. "What are you thinking?" asked Willow.

"Well, I want to use older people for a start. People your age and above. And have some of the action in the streets, not just in the church or hall. I thought the streets could be darkened, lighting off except for a few dim lights in windows, people bustling about the main street. It was a busy time and Bethlehem would be crowded. Then round the corner would come a couple more travellers, a man and a pregnant girl, with a donkey."

"A real donkey?"

"Yes, why not? I'm sure there's one locally that we could borrow. Anyway, they come to an inn – the Blue Boar – and knock on the door. The landlord comes out – no beds left. They go on to another, the Wheatsheaf maybe. Same story. So they try B&Bs. No room anywhere. By then Mary's having contractions, doubling up in pain. They've got to find somewhere pretty quick!"

"And it happens to be a stable," said Rachel. "By the way, I think I know where we can get a donkey. The people at the farm next to us have donkeys as well as horses. The farmer was really nice when he came to rescue us. I'm sure he'd lend one."

"That would be brilliant," said Sadie. "Anyway, I think the actual action would have to switch to somewhere else at that point. People couldn't crowd in to a stable to watch. Maybe we'd go to the church or the hall for the manger scene."

"Would the donkey go right inside?"

"No, I don't think so. He might get scared and out of control. We'd cut until after the baby is born. We could have the stage dimly lit and then the lights would go on to reveal Mary and Joseph and the baby in the manger. A lot will depend on lighting. For one thing, we'll have to get the street lights switched off for a little while."

And that was why Sadie was off to a meeting with the council people. We all hoped they'd co-operate and not be awkward and start raising objections, like Health and Safety or insurance and things like that.

"Say a prayer for me," said Sadie, putting on her coat and pulling a woolly hat down around her ears. It froze hard every night these days, after sunshine during the day, and a row of icicles formed round most house roofs by morning. No sign of a thaw any time soon. It looked like being a white Christmas.

"Josh and Abi are both fast asleep," she said. "With luck, they'll stay that way until morning. Abi does have a new tooth coming, so if she wakes and fusses, give her a spoonful of Calpol. There're nibbles and drinks in the fridge, just help yourselves. Make some hot chocolate if you like. A couple of new DVDs by the TV. Shouldn't be too late. Enjoy yourselves."

She was gone. The three of us looked at each other. Babysitting at the Vicarage was always fun, but seemed especially inviting this evening, with the sitting room curtains drawn against the night and a blazing fire, with shabby but very comfy sofas to sink into. We poured ourselves a Coke and tried to decide which DVD we'd watch first.

"Cushy number, this," said Amber, sinking into the red armchair. "And we get paid for it too! I must say I really love babysitting!"

three

The first hour was brilliant. We watched a cool movie in front of a blazing fire, with our feet up and our hands dipping into a box of chocolates Sadie had left with the other nibbles. Outside we knew it was freezing hard, but in here we were as cosy as bugs in a rug. We even remembered to do a little time of prayer, asking God that the council would have the right response to Sadie's ideas, because we were all getting quite keen on the Nativity play plans as well now.

Sadie hadn't yet decided about how much speaking there'd be, but if there were scripts to be written I was up for it. Amber was more interested in the casting, she didn't say so but I guessed she had thoughts about a leading role or, failing that, stage managing. Willow could see a few problems ahead; would it really be possible to get the whole of the town, or at least the main street, to co-operate? Would some of the grumpy ones raise objections, and take the attitude of Scrooge in *A Christmas Carol* that Christmas is all humbug anyway? What if the donkey bolted? What if everybody laughed? We were almost bending double in stitches ourselves thinking of Fred Parry, the landlord of the Blue Boar, standing at his door in a dressing gown and check tablecloth, shaking his head and saying "No room!"

We were just recovering our breath when I thought I heard a little sound from the baby alarm intercom. Then I was sure I'd been mistaken. It was only five minutes since I'd been upstairs to check on Josh and Abi in the sunny yellow nursery lit softly by a nightlight, Abi in her cot and Josh in his little bed. They'd been well away in the Land of Nod, two sleeping cherubs. Abi was clutching a tatty pink rabbit and Josh had a little plastic spanner held tight in his hand. His dad said he was sure

Josh would be an engineer or a motor mechanic one day. He'd never seen a boy so interested in nuts and bolts and the workings of things.

But there had been a noise. "I think I heard something," I said. "I'll go and check again."

But even before I could get out of my chair, there came sounds that all of us heard. The murmur of a toddler's voice, followed a second later by a pattering of feet, a sudden loud thump and a wail.

All of us were on our feet in an instant, scattering chocs everywhere from the overturned box, pounding up the stairs and along the passage. In the nursery, we saw what had happened in a moment. Abi must have stirred and woken, probably disturbed by her new tooth, and woken Josh. Josh had got out of bed, gone over to the cot and somehow managed to let down the side. Abi had fallen, or been pulled, out onto the floor. We saw with relief that she wasn't hurt, in fact her little face was beaming with delight at this unusual turn of events. She and Josh were on their feet in the corner by the toy cupboard, giggling and busily pulling out toys. They looked up in surprise when we burst in, but not alarmed at all. They know us well.

Willow was taking control. "Oh Josh, what are you doing? Back into bed, I think."

Amber went over and began to rearrange the tumbled cot covers. I saw a stubborn look cross Josh's little face. In that moment he looked remarkably like his mum when she's got an idea into her head. "No," he said firmly.

"Yes, you have to. Both of you. Come on, we'll tuck you in and read you a nice story."

But Josh, having gained extra play time, was not going to give it up easily.

"No. I play."

"We'll have to just grab them," said Willow. "You get Abi, Chloe, I'll see to this young man!"

I'd never have believed that a three-year-old and a 13-month-old who'd just learned to walk could move so fast. All three of us were there and ought easily to have managed the situation. But quick as a flash, Josh grabbed his sister's hand and the two of them headed for the open door. They went down the passage at a fast toddle, in a flurry of shrieks and giggles and small twinkling legs in animal-print pyjamas. Before we could reach them they'd got to the bathroom, scrambled inside and shut the door in our faces with a slam. Then we heard the ominous sound of a key turning in the lock.

Willow's face was pale. "Oh no! They've locked themselves in!"

She hammered on the door. "Josh! Open this door! Now! Do you hear?"

Silence from inside. Then a little sound from Abi that was half giggle, half whimper.

"We've got to get them out," said Amber, sounding panicky. "They could hurt themselves."

I was already having visions of little hands opening cupboards and finding bottles of bleach and cleaning stuffs and medicines. And then we heard another sound, the splashing of water on porcelain.

"They've turned the bath taps on," said Willow, sounding faint. "If the plug's in, it could fill up. Kids can drown in just a few inches – Josh! Open the door!"

No answer, just water running and a few bumps and thumps.

"What are they doing?" fretted Amber. "And what on earth are *we* going to do?"

We felt completely helpless, staring from each other's stricken faces to the firmly closed bathroom door. It was a solid door, one of the old original fittings that went with the house, stripped down to the wood, and had probably been around for centuries. No hope of breaking it down.

"Should we ring the fire brigade?" wondered Willow, whose control seemed to be slipping fast. "I think we'd better dial 999. Oh no, the phones are downstairs!"

"I'll get one," said Amber. More thumps, bumps, splashing and squeals came from inside the bathroom. Had Josh got Abi into the bathtub? Climbed in himself? Was it the hot tap or the cold tap that was running, or both? I prayed that the plug was not in place, and was dimly conscious that I was praying desperately all the time, help, help, help!

It was then that I got the idea. Amber had rushed off to get a phone. I stood close to the door and said, as loudly as I could, "OK, Willow, Amber's just gone to get the ice-cream!"

She caught on at once. "Oh, good, it's chocolate! I love choc ice!"

I thanked God that she'd remembered choc ice was Josh's favourite. There seemed to be a pause in the movements inside the bathroom. A listening pause. I said, "Here she comes! Oooh, it looks lovely!"

Amber was back with the phone, looking at me as though I'd totally flipped. I felt almost hysterical. "Oooh, yum yum! Delicious!"

It worked. We heard the key turn. The door opened slowly, and we saw two small figures, a little damp but unharmed, and two expectant little faces.

four

Getting them settled down again took quite a while. We took the children downstairs by the fire, dried them off and found clean pyjamas for them to change into. The two of them were all excited and hyper, it was a great novelty getting up again after being put to bed and they were going to make the most of it. Then we had to give them ice-cream, because Willow said you should never promise children anything if you're not going to carry it through. Luckily there was a tub of choc ice in the freezer. By the time they'd finished, their hands and faces needed washing all over again.

"I never knew childcare was such hard work," groaned Amber, flourishing a face flannel. "And there are three of us! How on earth does Sadie manage the two of them when she's all on her own!"

"I don't think I'll have any," I said. "Kids, I mean!"

The bathroom was a mess. We'd found that the bath plug was indeed in place, and that the bathtub was already half-full of freezing cold water. We shuddered to think of what might have happened if one or both children had toppled into it. Josh had decided to throw in everything he could lay his hands on – soap, soap dish, toothbrushes, the little plastic stool he stood on to use the toilet, and his dad's slippers, which had been left in the bathroom. He had managed to get the stopper out of a plastic bottle of bubble bath, and had poured that in too.

Abi had discovered a couple of spare toilet rolls and had obviously whiled away the time by pulling out yard after yard and festooning it around the washbasin, the laundry basket, the chair, and anything else she could reach. The other roll had been tossed into the bath to add to the collection there. Bits of damp toilet paper and wet puddles were everywhere. We did a cupboard count and thankfully, no dangerous substances had been touched. Fortunately, Rod and Sadie had all their medicines locked safely in a cabinet, and the bleach and cleaning things were stored on the highest shelf in the cupboard, well out of reach.

Amber and I cleared up and dried off as best we could, while Willow stayed with the children in their bedroom until they were both soundly asleep again, which took some time as they were well wound up and excited by their adventure. All of us were quite exhausted and rather subdued when we gathered in the sitting room again, with the intercom turned up high so we wouldn't miss the slightest sound.

"Rod and Sadie will be home soon," said Willow. "What on earth are we going to say to them?"

"They're not going to trust us with the kids after this, are they?" said Amber in a small voice.

I had this awful sinking feeling that we'd let Rod and Sadie down, big time.

"Maybe we don't need to tell them every single thing," Amber went on. "Couldn't we just say they woke and asked for ice-cream, and then we had to change their pjs? We wouldn't actually be telling any lies."

I thought Willow would jump in and squash this idea right away, but she was looking thoughtful and I knew she was weighing up the possibilities. We'd mopped up and cleaned up all the mess. We might just get away with it. Mightn't we?

Then I began to think again. What if they noticed things moved around in the bathroom and asked questions? How would we explain Rod's sopping wet slippers, for example? We could say Josh threw them in the bath, I suppose, and that would be true. But then she'd wonder why there'd been water in the bath and we'd have to invent a story about that. One fib would lead to another, and before we knew it we'd be lying through our teeth about everything. Josh could talk now, after a fashion; he might add his own account. We'd be in it up to our necks, and when the truth came out they'd certainly never trust us again. And they'd be right.

I took a deep breath. "I think we'll have to tell them. Everything."

Willow nodded. "Yes, you're absolutely right, Clo. Like they say in court, the truth, the whole truth, and nothing but the truth."

"So help me God," said Amber. "You're right. And we didn't even consider him, did we? God, I mean. What he'd want us to do. I mean, he did help us keep the kids safe. He wouldn't want us to go and mess it all up by telling lies."

"We'd better ask him to help us again, I think," said Willow. So we did, sitting on the rug in front of the fire and holding hands. Afterwards, I looked round the cosy, slightly shabby room lit by firelight and felt sad. I didn't think we'd be coming here to babysit again.

Not long afterwards, there was the sound of car wheels scrunching on the driveway and the slam of a door. Sadie blew in through the front door, we could feel the cold air even with the sitting room door closed. We heard her kick off her boots, then she poked her head round the door, said, "Hi, gang!" and ran upstairs to peek at the kids, which is what she always did when she came in. We looked at each other. The moment of truth was here.

As Sadie came back downstairs we heard the front door open again and voices in the hall. Rod was back too. They came in together, both their faces red from the freezing air. Sadie looked from one to another of us, slightly puzzled. "You're all very quiet, girls. No TV, no music. Is everything OK? I noticed Abi's wearing her Peppa Pig sleepsuit when I'm sure I put her to bed in her jungle animals one. Did she throw up? She sometimes does when she's cutting a tooth."

We looked at each other again. There was no wriggling out of anything now. We had to spill the beans.

"There's something we have to tell you," said Willow. "And I don't think you're going to like it."

five

Rod and Sadie both looked at us expectantly. They didn't seem particularly concerned, having seen that their kids were safe and well and that the Vicarage was still standing and not burned to the ground. They sat down side by side on the big sofa, and in spite of my quaking insides I couldn't help thinking what an unlikely vicar and vicar's wife they looked. Rod in jeans and a thick sweater, Sadie in a long flowing skirt, chunky cardigan and stripy socks.

Willow and Amber and I looked at each other again and Willow cleared her throat. And then she told them everything, sparing no detail, from the moment we'd heard the first murmur from the baby alarm to the moment they walked in the door. I cringed inwardly, and Amber was twisting her hands together in her lap, but Willow was quite relentless. The truth, the whole truth and nothing but the truth.

There was silence for a moment when she stopped speaking. I noticed that Sadie had gone pale when she heard that her children had been in real danger. Rod reached out and took her hand. "It's all right, love. Nothing happened to them." She smiled shakily and nodded. Rod turned back to us and said, "Is that it, then?"

Willow took another deep breath. "No, there's more."

Amber and I both looked at her in surprise. She'd told everything, surely?

"Afterwards," said Willow slowly, "we were wondering how to tell you and we talked about only telling you part of the story. Missing out a few things, the things that made us look bad. We were – we were almost planning to lie to you. Kind of."

"But you didn't," said Rod.

Willow shook her head. "No. But we almost did. We talked about it."

"But you didn't," said Rod again. "And we appreciate you being honest with us. Don't we, Sade?" Sadie nodded and he went on, "I'm sure I've said this before but I'll say it again. There's nothing wrong with being tempted, everybody is at some point or another. The wrong comes when we give in to it. We not only begin to feel guilty, but we lie and deceive to cover up, like Adam and Eve in the Garden of Eden, and we lose our self-respect and the trust of others. Sorry. I'm preaching a sermon and it's not even Sunday! But we're glad you were straight with us. Well done those girls!"

We managed a couple of weak smiles between us. This wasn't quite what we'd expected. Rod and Sadie looked at each other.

"As for those two rascals upstairs, maybe we've been a bit remiss there. There are a few things perhaps we ought to change," said Rod. "Like putting Josh in a room of his own. We've been thinking it was time to do that. Maybe it's time we acted on it."

"Yes," said Sadie. The colour had come back into her cheeks. "I've been meaning to mention that. They do tend to wake each other up if one is restless. I think we'd better move Josh's bed to the room across the landing, asap. Maybe tomorrow even."

"Who'd have thought the little monkey could figure out how to let Abi out of the cot though? And turn the key in the bathroom door. We'd better get a childproof lock, I think. He's getting way too clever for his own good," said Rod, sounding actually quite proud of his son. He laughed, and we all relaxed a bit. I couldn't quite believe it, but they didn't seem to be angry with us at all.

Willow said, in a small voice, "It was our fault really. We were responsible for them. There were three of us there, and we should have been able to stop them from running off."

Sadie laughed too. "Don't beat yourselves up about it! Those two can move like greased lightning when they want to – don't I know it!"

Amber blurted out, "But Rod's slippers are probably ruined!"

And then they both roared with laughter, until we couldn't help laughing ourselves.

"Don't worry about the slippers." said Rod. "I never liked them anyway. They were a present last Christmas from my great-aunt Dorothy and believe me, I'll be glad of an excuse to bin them!"

It was going to be all right. The tension had drained right away and I could feel tears of relief in my eyes.

"Of course," said Willow quickly, "you don't have to pay us for this evening. In fact, we ought to do a couple more babysits free of charge. That is – if you still want us."

"Of course we still want you!" said Sadie. "What in the world would I do without my Beech Bank girls?"

She got up and knelt on the rug beside us, and somehow managed to get her arms round all three of us for a hug.

"In fact," said Rod, "I think we ought to pay you a bit over the odds for this evening, to cover all the extra work you've had to do, all that mopping and tidying. OK, Sade?"

"OK," said Sadie, and gave us another hug.

It was getting late. There was a bleep on my phone; it was Peter, texting to ask when I would be getting home, as Auntie Sue was beginning to get her knickers in a twist. It was time to go. We got up and began the lengthy process of getting into our coats, boots, scarves, gloves and hats and venturing out into the chilly night.

"I'll run you home," said Rod. "You've had a stressful evening and the pavements are still a bit slippery."

We were heading out into the cold when Sadie called after us. "Oh, by the way, the evening was a great success. The council have agreed to co-operate with the lighting and everything else. So it's all go, and full steam ahead." She stuck up both thumbs.

When Rod dropped me at my gate I stood for a moment, looking at the stars shining in an inky black sky. The moon was almost full and the town lay under a blanket of white, mysterious and twinkling with points of brightness where surfaces sparkled with frost. God created all this, I thought, the moon and starlight and snow and frost, and the millions of stars stretching into unknown galaxies far into space. And yet he knew me, Chloe Wright, personally by my name, and watched over me night and day, knew all my comings and goings and even the number of hairs on my head. And time and again he worked out things for my good.

I could have stayed there for ages, despite the cold, looking up into the night sky and thinking about the vastness and wonder of it all. Someday, I thought, I would write an epic novel about the stars, and space, and the universe, and God.

But for now, I was brought back to earth by a sudden beam of light spilling out of our window and reaching across the front lawn. Auntie Sue had drawn back the curtain and was peering out to see if I was coming. My feet were beginning to feel cold now. I took one more look at the stars and then turned and walked up the front path and into the warm.

PART FOUR

Annie's Story

SHOPPING AND SURPRISES

one

Though I say it myself, I think I coped pretty well that day I sprained my ankle. I mean, I didn't scream, or sob (at least, only for a minute or two) or throw a wobbly and make a big deal out of it. The girls were brilliant, taking care of me and giving first aid. Rachel even gave me her scarf for a makeshift bandage, although it was freezing cold and she could have done with the scarf herself. My ankle was throbbing badly though, and I've never been so glad to see other people when that tractor came to rescue us.

Once I was home, the worst problem wasn't the pain, it was the boredom. I missed a few days of school, because I was supposed to keep my foot up most of the time. So for much of the day I was on my own, with Mum at work and Harry in school, watching daytime TV and playing computer games until my eyes had spots in front. The girls texted me and called by most days, but I spent long hours with only myself for company. Boring, boring, boring.

It was on the third morning that I got a phone call from Mum at work. She sounded a bit flustered. "Oh, Annie, I just got a message from the hospital. It seems they've put you in for a physio appointment, at short notice. This afternoon." She paused. "The thing is, I just can't get off from work to take you. They're short-staffed, lots of people can't get in because of travelling conditions."

"I could go on the bus," I said. "I'm sure I could manage."

"The buses aren't running," said Mum, "or at least, not a full service. I checked. I rang your dad, to see if he could come and get you. But he's up north at a conference, has been since before the snow came." She paused again. "But I did speak to Samantha. She's not at work today, and she offered to take you."

"What? No way! I'm not going with her!"

"But I thought you were getting on with her these days."

"We're OK. But I don't want to go off with her on my own."

The first time I'd met Samantha had been a total disaster, but that was mainly Dad's fault. Or maybe partly mine, if I'm honest. I'd convinced myself that Dad and Mum were going to get back together, and that Dad was planning to discuss it with me over lunch. Instead, he'd brought Sam along and introduced her as his new girlfriend. I'd been totally freaked out and humiliated, and I could see that she was upset too. Not that I'd cared about her feelings. It was only after I'd talked to Mum and then later to Sadie that I'd calmed down and got things a bit more into perspective.

Since then, I've met Sam a few times, but always with Dad and my brother Harry there too. It was a bit strained at first but was getting easier, mainly because Harry has no sense of relationship tensions and will get along with anybody, especially if food or outings or treats are involved. He chatters all the time and demands attention, which is OK because it provides a focus for the rest of us and makes it less embarrassing.

Being alone with Samantha though was a totally different ball game and one I wasn't sure I wanted to play. I said, "Mum, do I have to go? It won't hurt to skip this physio, will it?"

"Well, I don't know. It's important to get your foot back right. And appointments are hard to get. They only offered this one because of a cancellation."

"But Mum . . ."

"For goodness sake, Annie! Whatever your objections are, get over them! I'm going to call Samantha back and say you'll be ready at two. She's even got a little folding wheelchair that was her grandmother's, in case walking is difficult for you."

"Mum . . ."

"Two o'clock. On the dot." Click! And she was gone.

Well! I sat looking at the phone and feeling gobsmacked. I was definitely bored of being home, but not at all sure I wanted to have a girls' afternoon with Samantha. And certainly not be pushed around by her in a wheelchair! But when Mum puts her foot down, she means business. I heaved a sigh and reached for my crutches. I'd have to grit my teeth and get on with it, the physio, and the company. End of. I hopped over to the wardrobe and tried to decide what to wear.

Sam arrived in her green Volvo when I was still struggling into my coat. I'd managed to get into my Uggs, bandage and all. Samantha was looking rather gorgeous in a big red parka with fur round the hood, a white woolly hat, and black leggings tucked into red boots, also fur trimmed. I have to admit she's very nice looking and knows how to dress. Not for the first time, I wondered what she sees in my ordinary, middle-aged dad. Not his looks, that's for sure. His bank balance? Maybe, seeing that he has a plum job in his company, although he has to fork out maintenance now for us as well as his own expenses. But I didn't think it was that either. Sam has an executive job of her own.

I gathered up my crutches and hobbled down the path to the car, where she fussed about getting me fitted comfortably into the front seat. It all felt a bit surreal, me going off with Dad's fancy woman. I'd resented her like crazy at first, although Mum said I mustn't think of her as a home-wrecker, because the marriage was over long before she came along. But the knowledge of her made the loss of Dad seem more final somehow. He'd never belong to just Harry and Mum and me again.

Still, it was really nice being out and about, driving into the city and looking at the snow-covered verges and bare black trees and hedgerows standing in a landscape of white. Sam didn't talk much, the roads had been cleared but were still a bit tricky, and she drove carefully, keeping her eyes ahead. I noticed her hands on the wheel, she'd taken off her gloves and her hands were strong looking with oval nails. She had on deep red lipstick to match her coat, and I'd have expected her to wear some dramatic nail colour, plum or purple maybe, but she had them trimmed quite short with just a clear nail polish. She turned to smile at me and I looked quickly away. I didn't want her to think I was curious about her. Or even particularly interested. I was only doing this because I had absolutely no other option. End of.

two

It was a gloomy afternoon, but seemed much brighter when we got into town and saw all the lighted shop windows with their Christmas displays, and the street decorations and huge Christmas tree in the shopping centre. If it wasn't for this stupid ankle, the girls and I would be planning a mega Christmas shopping expedition, I thought regretfully. Shopping in a gang is a lot of fun, but not in Christmas crowds when you're on crutches. I had the feeling that most of my shopping would be done on-line this year.

In the hospital car park, Sam said she'd brought the

wheelchair along in the boot, just in case I needed it. I said no thanks. I had to admit though, it was quite hard work hopping across the car park and in through the big glass doors. But not as bad as being pushed by her.

We found the physiotherapy department without much trouble, but the appointments all seemed to be running late. The receptionist looked harassed and kept apologising to people for the delay. I sighed and tried to adjust my ankle so that it wasn't sticking out in everyone's way. The seats were blue fake leather and squeaked whenever you moved.

"They're very busy," remarked Sam. "Let's hope you don't have too long a wait."

"You don't have to wait with me," I said, and even as I spoke I realised how ungrateful I sounded. "You could go and have a coffee or something in the restaurant."

"It's OK," she said, not seeming to notice any rudeness on my part. "I thought maybe we could have a coffee together afterwards."

I shifted a little further away. I wasn't ready for girly coffee sessions with Sam just yet – if ever.

My foot was really aching now. I had to put it up by resting it against the back of the chair in front, but the person in the chair turned round and glared at me. I sighed and looked at my watch. Only four minutes since I'd last looked, but it seemed like an age.

"Actually," said Sam, "I'm glad of a chance to talk to you. We – your dad and I – have been wondering about Christmas arrangements."

I felt myself stiffen. I could guess what was coming. She and Dad were probably going to some swank hotel in an exotic place, to have a sophisticated grown-up Christmas. Never mind about me and Harry and Mum.

I gave a shrug without replying, and she went on, "Neil – I mean your dad – thought he'd like to spend Christmas with you and Harry and your mum, so you could have some time together. I plan on going to my parents in Edinburgh. That's where my family's from. I don't know if you knew I'm Scottish? I've lost most of the accent over the years."

I thought, no, I didn't know, and I'm not interested in where you're from, or your accent, or anything else about you. But I'd pricked up my ears at the rest of what she'd said. Part of me was still sore at the split in our family, though not as bad as I'd been, and was slightly indignant at the thought of them discussing and arranging our Christmas between themselves, and Dad swanning in and out of our lives whenever he felt like it. But there was another part that just longed and ached for him to be there, to be a complete family again, if only for a little while.

Sam must have sensed my confusion, because she said, "He'll discuss it with your mum and see what she thinks, of course. But it might be nice for you to have Christmas together."

I mumbled something about our arrangements not being settled yet. She nodded and seemed to understand.

"Is your ankle hurting?" she asked, as I shifted yet again trying to get comfortable. "You look a bit pale."

I had to admit that it was, and she said, "I'll go and see if I can hurry them up."

She got up, but before she was half-way to the reception desk there was a sudden commotion. Two young guys came bursting in through the swing doors, one with a makeshift bandage wrapped round his hand. They were in jeans and work boots, maybe workers from a building site. They were also very loud and a bit aggressive. I got the impression they might have been drinking a bit, even though it wasn't yet three in the afternoon. They pushed up to the desk, completely ignoring an elderly lady who seemed to be waiting for the receptionist to look up some details in the back. The old lady shrank back against the wall, looking nervous. The uninjured one slammed his hand on the bell and loudly demanded attention. "Can someone get out here please? My mate's cut himself."

The receptionist ran out, looking apprehensive. "How did he get this injury?"

"Never mind that. He needs to see a doctor, now. It's an emergency. This is A&E, right?"

"This is the waiting room for A&E, and other departments, yes. If you'd take a seat . . ."

The guy thumped his hand on the desk. "He's bleeding, I tell you! Needs to be seen. Now!"

The girl cast a quick look at the makeshift bandage. Even I could see that apart from a few streaks, there was no blood seeping through.

"If you'd just take a seat. I'm dealing with another patient." She turned to the little lady, who still looked scared to death. "Mrs Parsons, if I could just have . . ."

I couldn't believe it, but the aggressive guy actually shoved the old lady as she tried to go forward to the desk. There was a gasp from several of the waiting patients.

Next moment, Samantha was there beside her, facing the two young men with blazing eyes. "If I were you, I'd sit down and shut up! Your mate's in no danger. Take your turn. And I've a good mind to report you for assaulting this lady."

She put her arm round the elderly lady, who was shaking. I realised that I was holding my breath in amazement. I thought for one moment that the aggressive one was going to hit Sam, but the injured one pulled at his arm and muttered something about going elsewhere. They both turned and disappeared out of the swinging doors.

Sam was standing with the old lady, and when she'd finished at the desk, she guided her back to her seat. Then she came back and sat with me, breathing a little fast. A murmur of comment hummed round the waiting room. Sam looked at me and gave a little laugh. "Oh dear, I forgot to remind them about you. Sorry."

"It's OK," I said quickly. "It's not aching so much now." It was true, I'd quite forgotten about the pain in the drama of the moment. Sam went on, a little breathlessly, "It's just that I can't stand people being pushed around. And that lady reminded me of my gran. I looked after her for three years, the last three of her life. I was her carer. People can treat elderly people as though they don't exist, show them no respect. It makes my blood boil."

Her cheeks were pink, her eyes bright. I was looking at Sam in a totally different light. It was true what she said about old people. I'd noticed they often seemed to get shoved to one side. And I hated any kind of bullying too. I'd been bullied myself at my old school and I know just how helpless it makes you feel.

Just then my name came up on the board, and I had to get myself together and move. "Shall I come in with you?" asked Sam.

I shook my head, adjusting myself on the crutches. "No, it's OK." I paused, and then added, "But we could go for that coffee afterwards, if you like."

three

I hadn't really been looking forward to Christmas, I had to admit. I'd always loved it, especially the run-up to the big day. I'd loved the tacky advertising, the garish lights, even those awful inflatable Santas people have outside their houses, the shopping, the prezzies, the tree. Although I have to say that there'd been times, after the presents had been opened and we'd all stuffed ourselves full of food, that it all fell a bit flat and I wondered what all the fuss had been about.

This year I hadn't looked forward to it at all. At least we'd been a family last year, with Dad there carving the turkey and cracking silly jokes, and playing with Harry's new toys. This year everything had changed, new house, new district, new people. And no Dad. At least, that's what I'd assumed. I still wasn't sure what I really thought of Sam's idea of him spending Christmas with us. I couldn't quite picture it somehow. To be honest, I felt I'd much prefer to be with my friends, but of course they'd all be with their own families.

Mum was non-committal about the idea, said she needed to think very carefully and maybe discuss again with Dad. She thought Harry would love Dad to be there, but when she asked me what I thought, I just shrugged. I didn't know what to think.

She was more enthusiastic about another idea of Sam's though. Sam had decided it might be good for me to have her gran's folding wheelchair for as long as I needed it. I was doubtful, I mean, I'd be like an invalid! But Sam had said, well, give it a try anyway, see how it goes. So when she dropped me off at home after the hospital visit, she dropped off the wheelchair too.

"I think it's a very good idea," said Mum. "You know you've been told your ankle will heal quicker if you keep your weight off it. You might even get the girls to wheel you to Beech Bank."

So here I was next day, having been called for by

Willow and Rachel after school, being wheeled at breakneck speed along the slushy pavements. Rachel was pushing and I found it a bit hair-raising, especially when she practised doing wheelies on the corners and running when we got to the gentle slope of Beech Bank. We were all weak with giggling by the time we reached the centre, and I was feeling a whole lot better already.

At the doorway, we ran into difficulty because Beech Bank was still waiting for a disabled access ramp to be installed, and at present there were a couple of steps to negotiate. Fortunately Hugh was there, and came to the door.

"Hold on, girls. I'll give you a hand with that."

And he gave a hoist and a heave and expertly manoeuvred me, chair and all, up into the hall.

Hugh helps at BB, he's especially good with the boys. He organises their games and sports, takes them karting and ten-pin bowling and mountain climbing and is generally there for boy things. He's a quiet sort of man, middle-aged, doesn't say a lot, but you have the feeling you could depend on him in a crisis. Now, as he checked my feet were OK, I realised he was quite attractive for a man of his age. Dark hair cut short and beginning to turn grey, a determined kind of jaw and eyes with a twinkly look. I didn't know anything about Hugh, but I knew Rod and Sadie trusted him absolutely.

I thanked him, and we made for the coffee bar area, but we'd hardly got settled at a table when Sadie rounded us all up and ushered us into the big hall, boys and girls.

Sadie and Rod were both there, which meant there must be a grandma on babysitting duty this evening. Sadie said she'd got us all together for a reason.

"I want to run over the arrangements for the Nativity play. You all know the details, I suppose?" Some didn't, so she went through them again.

"I want to really focus on the reality of the birth of Jesus," she said. "We all know the story – baby born in a manger, angels visit shepherds with the news, shepherds come to the stable, wise men follow the star and bring gifts to the new king." She paused. "We take it all for granted, don't we? I want to emphasise how it must have really been. For the people involved, for their families, for the times they lived in. For instance, what it must have been like living in an occupied country at that time."

"I never knew it was an occupied country," said one of the boys.

"Yes," said Sadie, "Palestine was part of the Roman Empire then, along with a lot more countries. Caesar Augustus, their ruler, was taking an inventory of all the people in the Empire. That's why they had to be counted, for tax purposes. I don't suppose for one moment Joseph and Mary wanted to go to Bethlehem so close to the birth of their baby, let alone have him born in a stable."

"I thought it was because they were very poor," said Molly, a girl from Year Twelve.

"No, not at all. Joseph was a craftsman, a carpenter, well respected in Nazareth where he lived. They'd have been comfortably off. Not rich, but not poor either."

Sadie paused again, looking thoughtfully at us all. "Mary and Joseph were very special people, ordinary in many ways but quite outstanding in their faith. God must have seen those special qualities when he chose them to be the earthly parents for his son."

"Who's going to be them in the play?" asked Amber.

"Ah. I'm thinking very carefully about casting," said Sadie, looking us over again. "I'm praying that I'll choose the right people."

I wondered who they'd be. Holly would make a good Mary, I thought, pretty and graceful and with the big brown eyes you'd expect Mary to have had. Joseph – hmmm. I had to say that most of the boys at Beech Bank weren't all that dependable.

But Sadie wasn't saying yet. "I'm giving it a little longer. Couple of days, maybe."

"We're OK for the donkey, anyway," said Rachel. "I've asked Mr Banks at the farm, and he says he'll lend us Edward. He's really ancient and very reliable, as long as there are no sudden loud bangs. He doesn't like loud noises."

"It'll be quiet, hopefully. No traffic, the roads will be closed off for a little while. We'll have the main action here, I think, in this big room."

"Will the donkey be coming in?"

This raised a titter. "No," said Sadie. "Not fair on him, too scary with the lights and everything. He'll go off for a nice supper when he's done his bit."

Sadie was checking off notes on a big pad.

"What about baby Jesus?" asked Chloe. "Is he going to be a real baby?"

"I don't think we've got one just the right age," said Sadie. "It ought to be a newborn."

"My sister's got this doll," said Amber. "Life size and kind of floppy. It looks well lifelike."

"That might be just the thing," said Sadie. "Now then, some of the mums are kindly doing costumes. And speaking of mums – Annie, I think I just saw yours coming in."

I turned in surprise. Mum didn't usually turn up at BB. She waved to me from the doorway, and mouthed, "Thought I'd call by after work. Save the girls pushing you home in the dark."

"Do you want to go, Annie?" asked Sadie. I didn't really, I was enjoying being here. I began to wheel myself towards the door, but Mum said quickly, "I can wait a few minutes. No rush."

I rather wished Mum hadn't come, and hoped she wasn't going to be annoyed at being kept waiting. But I needn't have worried. When we'd finally finished our session, Mum was sitting at one of the red metal tables, quite relaxed, sipping coffee and chatting to Hugh.

four

The wheelchair was such a success that the girls suggested we take it, and me, on the bus to go shopping in the city the following Saturday. Mum thought that would be a brilliant idea, as this wasn't one of our weekends for seeing Dad.

"I can drive you in, if you like," she offered. "I'm planning on going to do some shopping myself while Harry's at Rowan's for the day. That's if you can all squeeze in, plus chair. How many of you are going?"

I thought we all were, which would mean we couldn't possibly get into Mum's car. Besides, I didn't say so, but it's more fun travelling on the bus when you're in a group. So I politely declined Mum's offer, and hoped she wouldn't offer to meet us for lunch because I felt that would be a definite no-no too.

There'd been no more snow, but no real thaw either, so we were still living in a white landscape once we were out of town. On Saturday, the girls manhandled me, and the wheelchair, on to the bus and we set off in high spirits. All of us were there, even Willow, who'd rearranged her Saturday job timetable. It was ages since we'd all gone into town together, and none of them seemed to mind that I had to be pushed everywhere. In fact, they all argued a bit over whose turn it was. And when we'd bought a few things, the wheelchair was very useful for transporting our bags as well as me.

Despite recession and the hard economic times we were in, the shopping centre was jam-packed with people shopping as if their lives depended on it. Everywhere seemed to be having pre-Christmas sales and special offers to keep people buying.

Most people were helpful when confronted by a girl in a wheelchair, they made way and stood back or even once or twice let me jump the queue. It wasn't long, however, before I experienced the downside of apparently being disabled. I noticed that some people frankly stared at me, while others looked embarrassed or even quickly looked away and seemed to pretend I didn't exist. I heard one woman say to another, "Poor thing – so young!" while others put on a kind of sad, pitying expression. I felt a dreadful urge to giggle, and could hardly keep a straight face. But it was well annoying too, like when we went for a coffee and the girl behind the counter seemed to think that just because I couldn't (apparently) walk, that I couldn't speak or think either.

"Would she like whipped cream on top?" she asked the others, and I couldn't help saying, in a snooty kind of voice, "Yes please, she would, and chocolate sprinkles as well if you don't mind."

I was beginning to be very glad I only had a sprained

ankle and wasn't permanently disabled, and to understand a bit of how frustrating it must be for those who were. Hardly anyone seemed to treat me just like an ordinary person.

The crowds and lights and razzle-dazzle of all the Christmas stuff were exciting for a while, but when we'd done most of our shopping and there was still time before the bus home, we thought we'd like to go somewhere a bit quieter.

"We could go up by the cathedral," suggested Chloe. "It's peaceful, and there are some nice little shops around there."

We took the short cut through the alleyway between M&S and Iceland, and crossed the road into the narrow little street that came out in the cathedral grounds. It had cobblestones, which made the wheelchair a bit tricky, but we bumped along taking it slowly, and it meant we had time to look at the interesting small shops. There was a baby boutique (very expensive), a map and compass shop, a printer's, and a little French-style bistro that no doubt had chairs and tables outside on the cobbles in the summer. The cathedral came into view at the end of the street, tall, grey and majestic, towering over the snow-covered grounds and the huddle of small streets and shops around it. From inside came faint strains of organ music.

"Shall we go in?" asked Rachel. "I don't think you have to pay."

I didn't think I'd ever been inside a cathedral before.

Inside, it quite took my breath away. Another world, I thought, stone walls soaring to high rafters, a hushed atmosphere, beautiful coloured glass windows with pictures of biblical scenes. We wandered slowly down the wide aisles, talking in hushed voices, looking at the different areas, the stone tombs with statues of knights and ladies lying with closed eyes and clasped hands on top, wall plaques of people long dead. There was a place that had a kind of box with lighted candles in holes in the lid, where you could light a candle and say a prayer. And then we came to a little corner that was quite different, with red rugs on the floor, coloured plastic kids' tables and chairs and lots of picture books and colouring books. I was surprised. Kids obviously spent time here.

"Do they still have services here then?" I asked.

"'Course," said Holly. "It's where some people go to church."

"And have for hundreds of years," said Willow.

It made me feel slightly dizzy, thinking of the thousands of people who had sat in those pews, the feet that had walked these aisles, right back through the centuries. And how on earth had they built this place back in those days, without modern technology? And built it to last all this time.

"They must have been good builders," I said.

"They were," said Chloe. "I've read lots of books about the Norman period. They had the finest craftsmen, masons, architects, everything. They wanted to glorify God."

I felt awed. The organist, hidden away somewhere,

was playing different music now, something I recognised as a Christmas piece. From the Messiah, maybe? I wasn't sure, but suddenly I felt uplifted, as though my heart was soaring towards God just like the walls of this cathedral. The busy, noisy, commercial town centre we'd just left seemed suddenly unreal and far away. One day it would all pass, even the cathedral itself, but God would remain for ever.

"We'd better go," said Amber suddenly. "It'll be time for the bus soon. We don't want to miss it."

I felt reluctant to leave the peace and majesty of this place and return to the real world but we had no choice. We had to hurry, and the ride over the cobblestones was bumpier than before. I was hanging on to the shopping bags to stop them spilling over, and Amber was pushing me, when I happened to glance in the window of the little bistro as we were passing. We had gone past in an instant, and nobody else had noticed anything. But I'd seen, just for a moment, two people at a table inside, laughing and chatting. They hadn't noticed us going by, but I'd seen their faces quite clearly. One was Hugh from Beech Bank, and the other was my mum.

five

I didn't say anything to the others, in fact, I didn't get the chance to say much at all, because we realised we were later than we'd thought, and we had to hurry to catch the bus. But I thought about it all the way home, while the others laughed and chatted. What on earth was going on? How long had Mum been meeting Hugh on the quiet? Hugh, of all people! I was tempted to say something to Willow when she was pushing me on the last lap from the bus stop to home, but didn't for some reason. I still couldn't get my head round it! People did have private lives of course and were entitled to them. But not *her*! She's my *mum*, for goodness sake!

She was home already when I got there, her car parked on the driveway. Willow didn't stay, but saw me safely inside and left. I parked the wheelchair in the hall and hobbled to the kitchen.

Mum was stirring soup at the cooker, and turned as I came in. She looked just the same as usual. Or maybe a bit more upbeat, if I really looked. She was very trim in black trousers and a cream jumper, her hair was flopping over her forehead and her eyes were bright.

"Oh, hello, sweetie! I thought you'd be here soon! Had a good morning?"

I said I had, and must have sounded a bit strange because she turned and looked at me as I sat down and stuck out my ankle. "Is it aching? Must have been quite tiring round the shops, even in a wheelchair. It was just heaving, wasn't it? I looked out for you, didn't see you girls anywhere."

But I saw you, I thought. I wanted to ask questions but didn't know how to start. Suddenly, it felt as though I was the adult and Mum the teenager with things to hide.

"Annie, are you all right? You seem awfully quiet."

I took a deep breath. "Mum, what's going on? I saw you in that coffee shop by the cathedral. With Hugh."

"Oh." She put down the wooden spoon, turned off the gas and came and sat opposite me. "I didn't realise you were round that way. I didn't see you."

Suddenly I felt near to tears. "Mum, why didn't you tell me you were seeing Hugh?"

She looked first puzzled, then seemed to get it. She reached over the table and took my hand. "Oh, Annie, it's not like that! You've jumped to the wrong conclusions. I hardly know Hugh, I only met him for the first time at Beech Bank the other evening."

"Then what . . ."

"Well, we talked for a bit then, and then I happened to bump into him in M&S this morning. We chatted a bit more, then he suggested we had a coffee in the coffee shop there. Only it was so noisy and crowded, so he said there was this quiet little place he knew just round the corner. So we went there. That's all."

I felt a bit confused but mostly relieved. It would have been terrible to find that Mum had been carrying on with someone behind our back. I realised suddenly what parents must feel like when their children get up to sneaky things. The thought made me giggle.

Mum seemed reassured. She got up to pour the soup and put two steaming bowls on the table, along with the crusty bread. I was suddenly starving.

"Mind you," said Mum, going to the fridge for butter and cheese, "it was very nice to relax and chat over a coffee. I hardly see anyone these days except for family and work. And Hugh is a very interesting person. Did you know he used to be an anthropologist? He's travelled the world in his day, been to some amazing places. He's a very clever man. But then he had the terrible experience of losing his wife and child in an accident. Poor man, he must have been heartbroken."

She actually had tears in her eyes. I was amazed she'd learned so much about him in so short a time. I'd been going to BB for months now and just took Hugh for granted as someone who could be relied upon to be always there.

"It was his faith that got him through," said Mum, and I thought, wow, they even got on to the God stuff. It must have been some conversation.

"And are you seeing him again?" I asked, hoping I was sounding casual.

"Well," said Mum, picking up her spoon, "as a matter of fact, he did ask if I'd like to go to a performance of Handel's Messiah the week before Christmas. They're putting it on at the cathedral."

I nodded. "I think they were rehearsing it yesterday. Are you going?"

"I said I'd think about it, that I'd really have to discuss it with you and Harry before I decided. What do you think?"

"Well . . ." I swallowed a spoonful of soup. What did I think? It was a bit mixed really. Part of me wanted to cling on to my mum, to resist any further change, to remind her we needed her, me and Harry, we'd lost Dad and we didn't want anything happening with Mum too.

The other part of me could see how silly this was, how childish. Mum had a perfect right to some life of her own, to some enjoyment and happiness.

"It's fine with me," I said. "You go if you like."

"Thanks, love," she said. "I knew you'd understand. You're really growing up."

Later, I went for a lie down, to rest my ankle, which still ached when I'd been up and about for a while, and to listen to some music. I was glad I hadn't made a fuss. Mum said I was growing up, maybe she was right. I was certainly seeing a lot of things in a different light. Realising that things were not always black and white, and that people were not always what they seemed at first glance. Sam, for instance – who'd have thought she'd put her career on hold and cared for her gran for three years. Or that she'd be feisty enough to stand up to a bully twice her size.

And Hugh, who seemed just a nice ordinary quiet man, but who'd done amazing things in his life and gone through terrible tragedies as well. You never knew, and you could never judge people until you got below the surface, that was what Rod and Sadie always said. And they were right.

My ankle was feeling a lot better, even though I'd been out and about all morning. Every day it was getting stronger and I was sure it would be fine again very soon. In time for the Nativity play, and Christmas Day. I still wasn't sure whether Dad would be spending it with us, but I hoped he would. Suddenly, I couldn't wait for Christmas to come!

PART FIVE

Rachel's Story

BODY IMAGE

one

I suppose I first noticed a problem at the fashion show we put on at Beech Bank back in the autumn, though I didn't recognise it as a problem at first. I was modelling some of the gear as a supporting cast to the top models (Sadie, Willow and Amber's sister Kim), and made a bit of a stir when my ankles wobbled in three inch heels and I lurched sideways and almost landed in someone's lap. I was well embarrassed, but my sister Ruth was so mortified that you'd have thought I'd stripped off and streaked along the red carpet!

"I didn't know where to look! Everyone knows you're my sister, they might think I'm an idiot as well!" she told me later that night when we were getting ready for bed. The Steps were arriving next day, so Ruth and I were sharing that weekend.

I thought that was a bit of a cheek. "Nobody minded. They had a good laugh," I said.

"Yes, exactly! It's so not cool having a sister who's a laughing stock!"

I was getting a bit fed up of this conversation, and jumped into my bed. "Well, sorry I'm sure! Now let's forget it."

Ruth couldn't leave it alone though. "What on earth were you thinking, wearing those stupid six inch wedges? You might have known you couldn't walk in them!"

"Three inch, actually. And you know very well what I was thinking. That it would make my legs look longer. I just hate having short legs."

Ruth sniffed and pulled the duvet up to her chin. She said grumpily, "You'd really have something to worry about if you had my problems."

By this time I was in no mood to ask what she meant, and besides, I was tired.

"Yeah, yeah," I said. "I'm going to sleep now." And switched off the bedside lamp.

Ruth had always been so good natured, and I didn't like this new, moody, almost-thirteen-year-old sister. I wanted the old one back. It didn't occur to me until later to wonder what she'd meant by that last remark.

The next thing that struck me as odd happened weeks later, when the Steps had been for the weekend and we were getting back to normal, or what passes for normal round here. There are four of them, Ted's children from his first marriage, Max, who's between me and Ruth in age, twins of nearly eleven, Ben and Jade, and Billie, who's seven. We all get on pretty well, considering. The big downside when they come is that we have to shuffle sleeping arrangements around; Ruth comes in with me so the girls can have her room. The boys take up the spare room. What happens when the baby comes is anybody's guess.

Anyway, they'd been, and I was moving Ruth's stuff back into the girls' room. None of us are exactly tidy, and she is messier than most. I picked up an armful of clothes, bags and magazines to dump back in her room, and one of the mags dropped onto the floor. I dumped the stuff on her bed and went back to pick it up. She and Jade read a lot of teenage girlie stuff, mostly the sort that give away free gifts like sparkly hairbands and mini make-up kits. This one was a bit different, more for older girls, with a lot of emphasis on exercise, posture, diets and fashion. It was open at a page with headlines that said "Lose a stone by Christmas". I sat down and read the article. It was quite sensible I suppose, especially for people who are a bit overweight and unfit, giving a diet plan with emphasis on healthy eating – fruits, veg, carbs and proteins in proper balance. But as I was turning a page, a piece of paper slipped out, covered in Ruth's handwriting. It seemed to be a kind of diet plan. But I noticed right away it wasn't following the guidelines listed in the magazine, but that she'd made up her own, much more drastic, one. It read:

* * *

Breakfast: *small* amount of cereal, no sugar. Or fruit.
Lunch: Skip, if poss. Or small salad. Or yoghurt.
Tea: Same as family, small portion. Fruit. NO pudding.
NO: sweets, choc, biscuits, cake, crisps, fast food, fizzy drinks, snacks.

* * *

I sat and looked at the list. Was Ruth serious about following this diet? Did she think she was overweight and needed to lose a stone at least? She's a small girl and slightly on the chunky side, but then so am I. I might moan about my lack of leg length but I don't think I'm overweight. Obviously she did. It was a pretty drastic diet plan she'd worked out for herself. Was she serious about this?

I was still sitting on the bed looking at it when Ruth came in, took one look at the magazine and the list and went red as a beetroot.

"That's my private stuff, if you don't mind," she snapped, and snatched the list from my hand.

I felt I couldn't let it pass. She's my younger sister, after all.

"Ruth, you're not doing this stupid diet, are you?"

She looked even crosser. "I'm doing healthy eating, if you don't mind. It's what they teach us at school, isn't it?"

"Yes, but this is going OTT. You're cutting out just about everything."

"Only the junk stuff, if you'd take the trouble to read it properly. Fats and sugars and things with additives."

"But why? You must be half starving yourself!"

"'Cos I want to, that's why! It's my body, and I don't want to be a fat pudding all my life, so I'm taking control."

"But this is way too strict. And you don't need to lose weight. You're not fat."

"I'm fatter than I want to be. And you could do with losing a few pounds yourself."

She stomped off to her own room. I felt gobsmacked. What on earth had got into her? Could it be anything to do with the fact that Jade and Billie were showing every sign of growing up to be tall, leggy, blondes, all the things Ruth and I were not? I sighed. Ruth obviously wasn't prepared to listen to anything I said anyway, so I might as well save my breath. And maybe her diet sheet wasn't that bad anyway, it seemed to have most of the required nutrients, and it included an evening meal with the rest of us. I decided I wouldn't say anything to Mum just yet. It was probably just a fad she'd grow out of anyway, especially when Christmas came with lots of yummy mince pies, iced cakes and boxes of chocs.

I did keep an eye on Ruth at mealtimes though. She soon twigged, and took to glaring across the table at me. Her portions of breakfast cereal were tiny. I didn't know what she ate at school dinner, because we were both with our own friends. I breathed a sigh of relief when teatime came at home, because Ruth had a good plateful of spaghetti bolognese with the rest of us.

But after a few forkfuls, she asked Mum if she could take it upstairs to finish, as there was something she wanted to see on TV that the rest of us didn't watch. Mum agreed. She was quite absent-minded these days, which Willow said often happened with pregnant women, though how she knows that I can't imagine. Anyway, off went Ruth.

I was smelling a rat by now, because I realised that Ruth had done this several times lately. Later, when she was in the bath, I sneaked into her room and had a snoop around. Sure enough, when I looked under the bed, there was her plate of spaghetti bolognese, hardly touched. I looked around a bit more, and my heart sank to my boots. In the corner behind the dressing table I found the remains of yesterday's sausage and mash, and on top of the wardrobe, a mouldering plate of cauliflower cheese and gammon that must have been at least a week old.

It was then that I realised that Ruth had a real problem.

two

My own big problem now was, should I tell Mum about my worries or should I try to get Ruth to see sense by myself? That would be no easy thing. We'd always been good friends, but just lately she was acting as though I was Public Enemy Number One.

All the same, I didn't want to worry Mum.

Mum was particularly happy at the moment. We'd had such dreadful times when my dad was ill and when he died, and Mum had been sad and lonely for a long time afterwards. Meeting Ted had brought her to life again, all his kids loved her, and a new baby on the way was like the icing on the cake. She and Ted were over the moon, soppy as anything, when they thought we couldn't hear. They called each other embarrassing names, like "my little dumpling" and "Teddybearkins" which was enough to make one vomit. I'd had a few problems with the Steps and so on, but was over them now. I'd never have thought Ruth would be the one to cause hassle with an eating disorder.

I forgot the eating problems for a little while when the snow came and we had the accident out sledging and got marooned. Then we had the idea of borrowing a donkey for the Nativity play from Mr Banks, the farmer near to us. We'd made enquiries, and Mr Banks had been agreeable and asked Ruth and I if we'd like to go across and meet the donkey in question. We planned to go on the following Saturday, walking across the fields. We'd been several times to ride his horses. Mr Banks' son does the main farming, Mr Banks senior is semi-retired and his hobby is looking after horses who've been retired from work too, and sometimes donkeys as well. We had no Steps with us that weekend, and we looked forward to the visit.

The sun was shining outside that morning, but it was still bitterly cold. Mum made us porridge for breakfast, thick and creamy with maple syrup and chopped nuts on top.

"Fuel to keep out the cold," she said.

Ruth pulled a face at the amount in the steaming bowlful Mum put in front of her. She looked at me and glared as she picked up her spoon.

"No tricks," I said, when Mum had gone out of the room for a moment. "You eat it all, or you're not coming with me."

She had no choice really. She loves those animals of Mr Banks'. She ate the whole bowlful, glowering and looking as though it was poison. Afterwards she put her hand on her stomach and said, "Oh, yuck, I'm so full now. I feel blown up like a balloon. Totally gross."

"Tough," I said. "Come on, let's get our wellies and get going."

It was beautiful out of doors, crisp and sparkling, blue skies and sun reflecting so brightly off the snow-covered fields that it hurt our eyes. Ruth's mood picked up a little when we were out of doors. Or maybe it was the good breakfast she'd had. At any rate, she seemed almost like her old self again by the time we'd trudged through deep snow down the gentle slope that led to the farm nestled between two hills. All the farm animals were tucked up snugly in the buildings with plenty of straw to sleep in and mangers full of hay. The donkey, Edward, was in part of the stables, which felt warm with the heat of horses and had that lovely smell of hay and horse. Edward looked at us and blinked, with a long wisp of hay dangling from his jaws. He had long light-coloured eyelashes and a gentle expression.

"Think he'll do?" asked Mr Banks. "He was a seaside

donkey for years, you know. He's well used to carrying someone on his back."

I rubbed Edward's head and stroked his soft grey ears. He looked at me patiently from amber-coloured eyes. I thought of the hundreds of children who'd had fun riding on his back.

"Jump up, Ruth, and see how he feels about being ridden again," said Mr Banks, slipping a halter over Edward's head. Ruth scrambled up and sat on Edward's back. He turned his head and looked round with a slightly puzzled expression, as if to say, "I thought I'd done with all this", and then turned back to munching his hay. Ruth slipped off and stroked the dark, cross-shaped mark that stretched along his back in contrast to the lighter grey.

"I wonder why donkeys have a cross on their back," she said.

"It's because our Lord rode a donkey on his way to the Cross of Calvary," said Mr Banks. "Or so they say."

I hadn't heard that before. But, thinking about it, I realised that donkeys had played an important role in the life of Jesus. A donkey had carried his mother to Bethlehem before he was born, and he had ridden on a donkey, maybe the same one, when he went to Egypt to escape cruel Herod. And I remembered the donkey that Jesus had ridden on his last journey to Jerusalem, where he knew the cross awaited him.

There must be something special about donkeys, I thought, looking at Edward's gentle expression and patient eyes. They're small and humble, not strong and powerful like horses, yet they've been chosen to carry a king. They've got the most awful raucous voices, and I knew some could be stubborn and cantankerous, yet they'd been singled out for special honours.

"Do you think he'll do then?" asked Mr Banks.

"I think he'll be amazing," I said, and gave Edward's ears another rub.

On the way home up the hill, I noticed that Ruth seemed to be having difficulty keeping up with me. It was a bit hard going through the snow, but not that hard. She fell behind and I waited for her. "You OK?"

She seemed to be breathing hard, and looked crossly at me. "'Course. Why shouldn't I be?"

No point in picking an argument on such a lovely day, I thought. But I felt that small twinge of worry again.

three

It was a day or two afterwards that I got a chance to talk to Sadie at Beech Bank. Ruth came to BB as well now, quite often, and had come that afternoon. She and some others were playing table tennis in the games room while I finished my homework. Sadie was busy, moving from group to group, making plans with all of us, including two or three of the mums who'd offered to make angel costumes for the play. There were to be a lot of angels, apparently. She came to grab a coffee just as I finished my work and went to get one myself.

"Hi, Rach. Everything OK with you?"

I hesitated. I'd already told her about visiting Edward, and she was chuffed about that. Everything was coming together nicely. I had a sudden urge to tell her my worries about Ruth, but she was so busy I didn't quite like to. Besides, Ruth was right there in the building and could come by at any moment.

She noticed my hesitation. "Rachel? Anything bothering you?"

I still couldn't quite bring myself to mention my sister. I stirred my coffee, and said, "Sadie, would you say I'm too fat?"

She looked at me and then sat down with her own mug, though I'm sure she'd been planning to drink her coffee on the run. "Whatever makes you ask that?"

I shrugged. "It's just – well, I'm not like Chloe or Willow or Holly. Or Annie and Ams for that matter. They're all different, but they're all, well, kind of gorgeous in their own way."

"And you think you're not?"

I shrugged again, and said, "Well, I'm small, and kind of chunky, and most clothes don't look as good on me as on them."

Sadie looked at me thoughtfully for a moment. Then

she said, "Rachel, what do you see when you look in the mirror?"

I was surprised by that. "Well, I guess I see this round face, dark eyes, dark hair, kind of chunky figure. And short legs."

"And you don't like what you see?"

"Well . . ." This conversation wasn't going quite the way I'd expected. To be honest, I don't actually dislike myself that much. Except my legs. I'd been trying somehow to work round to Ruth's problems, without being too obvious. And it wasn't quite working out.

I shrugged yet again, and said in a non-committal way, "I don't know really."

Sadie put down her mug. "OK. Now I'll tell you what I see when I look at you. I see this lovely young girl, with pink cheeks, a friendly smile showing perfect teeth, and beautiful thick, shiny, dark hair. And your eyes. Did you know you have the most beautiful eyes, Rach? Like dark brown velvet, with the kind of long dark eyelashes most of us would die for."

I blinked. I'd never quite have put it like that, but I supposed she was right. She'd managed to focus on all my best features. There were still the bad ones though.

"As for your legs, well, they're fine – I don't suppose anyone else would even notice that they're short. And the way you dress can do marvels for making you make the most of your shape, choosing the clothes that really flatter you."

"It's OK for you," I said. "You've got the perfect figure.

Anything looks good on you."

She laughed. "When I was your age I hated being tall and skinny. It's not all good news. For instance, I have this terrible bony sticking-out collar bone, real salt-cellars. I can never wear low necklines. Whereas you have the kind of neck and shoulders that looks great with scoop necks and to show off nice jewellery. It's a real bind trying to find trousers that aren't too short in the leg, or tops that give me a bit of shape. I'd much rather not be straight up and down. But nothing I can do about it, that's the way I am. And you're the way you are. An endomorph."

"What?" I sat bolt upright in surprise. "What on earth's that? It sounds horrid, really freaky!"

She laughed again. "Just a name for your kind of body shape. I'm an ectomorph. So's Willow. Maybe Chloe too. I'd say the others were mesomorphs, or a mixture. Look, I'd love to stay and chat but I'm so busy. Why don't you look those names up on Google? It'll explain the different body types. And there's a link to a site with advice on how to dress to the best advantage for your body type."

She got up and dumped the mug in the sink. "Remember one thing, Rach. God created you, and he made you just the way he wants you. There's not another like you in the world. You and Ruth are very much alike, but not exactly the same. Not even identical twins are, their fingerprints are always different. You're unique. And you're the way God planned you to be. Beautiful!"

She was gone, swooping over to the snug where a couple of mums were looking at samples of white material for angel costumes.

I finished my own coffee thoughtfully. There are a row of computers in the quiet room, and usually they're all in use, either by someone doing homework or researching for a project. We're not encouraged to play computer games or do social networking at BB. Now, however, I saw that one was not being used, so I went over and googled the word *endomorph*. It came up with a whole lot of info on the different body types, and it was fascinating stuff. I looked at *endomorph* and *ectomorph*, and *mesomorph*.

A lot of things made a lot of sense. I learned, for instance, that ectomorphs – Sadie and Willow's body type – are likely to have fragile bones and not as much muscle power as others. They feel extremes of heat and cold more. Mesomorphs have large bones, strong muscles and they tan well. Endomorphs are round and soft, their limbs tend to be short and they have soft smooth skin. Many people are not purely one type but a mixture.

I could see very clearly now that Ruth and I were definitely endomorphs and so was Mum. Nothing we did would change our basic body shapes. There was a link on one of the sites leading to another that gave advice on the most flattering ways for the different types to dress. I had just clicked on it when a sudden commotion came from the games room. Someone screamed and there was a babble of voices. I saw Sadie go rushing across. Next moment Willow came from somewhere and was by my side, touching my arm.

"Rachel, you'd better come. We need to get hold of your mum. Ruth seems to have fainted."

four

It wasn't just an ordinary faint either, with Ruth crumpling to the floor. She had banged her head on the way down and was out cold.

There was pandemonium for a few minutes. Sadie was checking Ruth's breathing and taking her pulse. Hugh was trying to keep the others from crowding round. Ruth's friend Helen was sobbing. They let me through and I knelt down beside her. My sister's face was white as a sheet and my own heart was pounding. Sadie put a reassuring hand on my arm. "Try not to worry too much, Rachel. Her breathing's OK and her pulse steady. Hugh's sent for the ambulance. It'll be here soon."

The ambulance came almost at the same time as Mum and Ted in the car. Mum looked pale and frightened, Ted was trying to keep her calm. The ambulance crew quickly took control.

"Mild concussion, I'd say. We'll whip her off to the hospital, just to be on the safe side. Look, she's beginning to move her head. That's a good sign."

Ruth's eyes were flicking open and she moaned a little. The ambulance woman said, "Ruth, my name's Marie and I'm a paramedic. You've had a bump on the head and we're going to pop you into A&E for a check. Just lie still and don't worry about a thing."

They expertly got her on to a stretcher and into the ambulance, and motioned Mum to go along too. She gave Ted an anxious look, and he said reassuringly, "We'll be right behind in the car. Come on, Rachel."

The drive through the darkness, following the ambulance, was surreal and seemed to take ages, although we were driving quite fast. Ted glanced at me.

"OK, Rach? Any idea what made her pass out?"

I shook my head. Everything had happened so fast and I felt stunned and unreal. And then I realised I did know, or at any rate had a good idea. I said shakily, "Except that I don't think she's been eating properly."

He was silent for a moment, then said, "She's not on some slimming thing, is she?"

I glanced at him. Ted and I didn't often get the chance to talk about personal things. I wondered if he'd noticed Ruth's eating, or lack of it, even if Mum hadn't.

I said, "Well, she does have this idea that she needs to lose weight."

I half thought he'd tell me that this was all her own fault, then. But he was silent for a while again, and then said, "You and Ruth are going to be just like your mother." I hadn't expected that, and wondered what he was getting at. Then he said, "You know, your mother is the most beautiful woman. I've thought so from the first moment I saw her. And you and Ruth are growing up to be beautiful women too."

He didn't say any more, concentrating on driving between the verges of piled-up snow, grubby and grey from the passing traffic. I was silent too, taking in what he'd said. A lump came into my throat, because I suddenly remembered my dad, and the way he'd called Ruth and me his little princesses. My dad had thought we were beautiful too.

When we got to the city we had to stop at three lots of red lights, while the ambulance sped on ahead to the hospital. By the time we got there, Ruth had been taken inside. The A&E department was just like the ones on the TV hospital dramas, a kind of controlled busyness with people on the move, rubber soles squeaking on shiny floors, nurses and doctors in their scrubs nipping in and out of cubicles, the swish and rattle of curtains being pulled round or drawn back, someone moaning. We found Ruth in a cubicle at the far end, propped up on a bed and already conscious, a bit pale and bemused to find herself here. Mum was beside her, looking relieved.

"They say she's fine, nothing damaged, but they'll keep her in overnight for observation as she was unconscious for a while. The doctor'll take a look at her when he has a minute. They're so busy here."

"That's good news," said Ted. "Bit of a sore head then, Ruth?"

Ruth gave a sheepish kind of grin and touched her head. "I've got the most ginormous bump coming up. Feel it, Rach."

I felt it. It was certainly impressive. But I could also feel the fear and tension draining away from us all. She was going to be OK.

"Tell you what," said Ted. "Why don't we get a cup of tea while we're waiting for the doc? The restaurant's probably closed, but I'm sure there's a machine somewhere. Want one, Rachel?"

I shook my head. "No thanks. I'll wait here with Ruth."

Alone, I tried to decide what to say to her. Should I mention the reason for the fainting? I didn't have to, because she spoke first.

"I know what you're going to say. That I passed out because I skipped lunch."

"I didn't know you had. But yes, I bet that was why. You get low on blood sugar if you don't eat, and that's what happens."

"OK, you needn't read me a lecture. Are you going to tell Mum?"

I hesitated. I didn't want to say I'd already told Ted, and that he was probably passing the information on to Mum this very minute. Yet I couldn't let this go on. She was putting herself and her health in danger.

She was quiet for a bit, tenderly fingering the lump on her head. Then she said, in a quiet little voice, "It's a bit scary really."

I said quickly, "But you're all right, Ruth. No real damage done."

"No, I mean the eating thing." She looked away from me, picking at the blue cover they'd put over her. "I thought it made good sense when I started the eating plan. I thought I would kind of take control, make myself look the way I wanted to. But it's not working. I think I've lost a bit of weight, but I'm getting to feel sometimes I can't eat even if I'm hungry. My throat kind of closes up. It's – it's kind of controlling me now. And my shape isn't really changing."

A tear slipped out and slid down her cheek. I wanted to put my arms round her and hug her, but I didn't think she'd like it. I said, "Ruth, you can't change your shape by what you eat. You and me, we're both endomorphs."

"What?" Ruth's eyes opened wide. "Endo what? Are you trying to be funny? Are you saying we're some kind of aliens from another planet?"

"Don't be silly, it just means a type of body shape. I've been looking it up on the Internet. But I really think you ought to tell somebody about this eating thing. You don't want to keep passing out and ending up in here, do you?"

"No, I don't. I hate this place! I want to go home, now."

"They're only keeping you in for one night. But I wish you'd get some help. Maybe there's someone in the hospital you could talk to. They're going to want to find out why you fainted, anyway."

She looked dubious. "I don't want Mum to know. She'd worry. You won't tell her, will you?"

I was in a dilemma now. I just didn't know how to answer, but at that moment Mum and Ted appeared from the direction of the lifts. I looked at their faces anxiously, wondering what had been said, but they weren't giving anything away.

Mum said, "Oh, you're looking much better Ruth, you've got some colour in your cheeks. I just saw the doctor, he's on his way here now. He'll check you over, and if all's well they're going to bring you some soup and a sandwich."

I saw a kind of scared look flit across Ruth's face. Mum had sat down again, and Ted was beside her. I stood back a little and next time Ruth glanced my way, I mouthed silently, "Eat it!"

five

I went to school as usual next day, but gave Beech Bank a miss afterwards, because I wanted to get home and see my sister. By the time I got there, she had already arrived. Mum told me she was upstairs taking a nap, because she'd had a bad night in hospital.

"Poor old Ruth," said Mum with a smile. "She said that

although they put her in a side room on her own, there were people walking up and down all night long. And a street light shining in right outside her window. The bed was hard as nails and she couldn't get comfortable. The heating was turned too high and she was boiling hot. She reckons she never slept a wink."

I grinned. All these complaints sounded as though Ruth was back to her usual self.

"She's OK, though?" I asked.

"She's fine. No ill effects."

I hesitated, wondering if the eating problem had been mentioned. Mum must have read my mind. "I gather you knew she's been missing meals and put herself on a so-called diet?"

I felt myself going red. "Yes, I did know. I'm sorry, Mum, I should have told you. I didn't want to worry you, but I'd have said something if I'd known she was going to make herself ill."

"It's not your fault," Mum said quickly. "The rest of us didn't notice anything. Maybe Ted and I have been a bit too preoccupied with the new baby coming. Anyway, Ruth's had a scare, and she knows how silly she's been. A counsellor at the hospital had a chat with her this morning and then she talked to me. Apparently they feel the problem has probably been nipped in the bud."

Mum sat down by the table and looked thoughtful. "The counsellor seemed to think that Ruth's been affected by the changes that have happened over these past few years – losing your dad, moving, me marrying Ted, the Steps, now a new baby on the way."

"But Ruth's chuffed about the new baby, and she likes Ted and the Steps," I said.

"Yes, but it's all change. Bad or good, it's all been outside her control. Managing her body image was something she thought she *could* control. Maybe even delay her growing into an adult, with all the things that seem to happen to adults. Although I don't suppose she consciously thought about it like that or realised what was happening."

"Poor old Ruth," I said.

"Yes," said Mum. "She's in need of a bit of extra TLC just now, I think. Why don't you take a cup of tea up and see if she's awake?"

Ruth was awake, and looked pleased to see me, though she wasn't going to admit it. She said, "I'm really bored. I'm going to school tomorrow, whatever Mum says. Hospital was gross. I thought I'd never get out of there."

I handed her the tea. My sister was truly back to her old self.

I wondered if I'd better mention the eating thing, but she was one jump ahead. "Don't start on at me either. You've been nagging me for weeks."

I was tempted to say, well, maybe you should have listened, but I didn't want to start a quarrel, so kept my mouth shut. She went on, "You needn't worry, I've done with all that."

She put the mug down on the bedside table, climbed out of bed, rummaged about in her top drawer until she found the diet sheet, ripped it up and dumped it in the bin.

"There! Now you can shut up and stop lecturing me."

I'd hardly said a word yet, but I kept my lips tightly closed. Ruth took a slurp of tea and glared at me.

"What's the matter? Why aren't you saying anything?"

"Chance would be a fine thing," I said. "You haven't let me get a word in yet."

And then suddenly we were both overcome by giggles, and Ruth had to put her tea down again because she was in danger of spilling it.

Suddenly I remembered something Sadie had said. I picked up the hand mirror from the dressing table and went to sit by Ruth on the bed, holding up the mirror in front of our two faces.

"What do you see when you look in here?"

Ruth looked from her reflection to me and back again. "What are you on about now? I see us. You and me. What else?"

I took a good look at the two of us. We were obviously sisters, but we were not exactly alike. Our noses were different, my face was slightly rounder and I had a dimple in my cheek while Ruth had one in her chin. But it was true what Sadie had said. Both of us had thick, dark, shiny hair, and pink cheeks, though Ruth was maybe a little paler than usual. And we did have lovely eyes, large and dark, with long curling lashes. I blinked mine, once or twice.

"We're truly beautiful," I said.

Ruth looked at me as though I'd flipped. "You're truly nuts, that's what I think." She bent to pull on her slippers.

"You know that website you were talking about, the one that gives advice on clothes for different body shapes. Could we have a look at it?"

"'Course. I'd like another look myself." A thought struck me. "We'll probably get money for Christmas, Granny and some of the aunties always give us some. Maybe we could look at the site and plan out new wardrobes, then go shopping in the sales. Get stuff that really suits us, not just what everybody else is wearing."

She looked pleased with that idea, and we gave each other high fives.

"And no more diets?" I said.

"No, I hated it anyway. I was hungry all the time but scared of food at the same time. And I really missed all the yummy stuff. Crazy. By the way, what's for tea?"

I tried to remember the ingredients Mum had in front of her on the kitchen counter.

"Spaghetti bolognese, I think. With cheese on top."

"Sweet!" she said. "My favourite!" and gave me another high five for good measure.

Ruth was back at school next day and back at Beech Bank as well. Sadie had her casting list now, and was going to run through it with all of us. We were puzzled, though, because none of us had been given scripts.

"Will we have time to learn our lines?" Amber asked.

"No lines," said Sadie. "This is a non-speaking production."

That surprised us. Amber looked disappointed, the rest of us relieved. The cast list was a surprise too. Nearly everybody was either an angel or part of the tax-paying crowd gathering in Bethlehem. There was a very lifelike baby doll to play the part of Jesus. Not even any shepherds or wise men. Basically only Joseph, Mary and the donkey. It was all going to be very simple.

"I've thought very carefully about this," said Sadie. "For Joseph, we need someone brave, steady and trusting in God, the kind of person Joseph was. So, if he'll agree, I've chosen Peter Wright."

There was a little flurry of surprise and interest. Chloe's brother Peter didn't often come to BB; he was older than most of us here. But I could see at once that he'd be perfect. Peter was facing an uncertain future with great courage, and he had a strong and positive faith in God that was getting him through.

I jumped when Sadie spoke again. "As for Mary, we thought Ruth would be just right. Dark hair and eyes, like Mary would have had. Small enough to ride a donkey, and someone who knows a bit about riding and won't be likely to fall off or be nervous. What do you think? Ruth, are you up for it?"

I was right across the room from Ruth, but even so I

could see her face light up with surprise and delight. For a moment our eyes met, and if we'd been near enough we'd have given each other yet another high five.

PART SIX

Willow's Story

CHRISTMAS IS COMING!

one

As Christmas approaches each year, my mother begins to look around for someone to come and spend it with us. Or several people. Sometimes it's relatives, but more often than not she also finds people who are lonely, or away from home, or who Mum thinks ought to be with a proper family over the festive season.

One year, it was a couple of Japanese students who spoke very little English, but were terribly polite, and bowed and smiled every time we met around the house. By the time they left, we were all bowing and smiling too.

Then there were two women from the local refuge, who came with five children between them, very destructive children who ignored the toys we'd bought for them and played with Rowan's and mine, managing to break most of them, or use up the batteries, or lose vital parts. There was a homeless man one Christmas who was very smelly, and thought it was weakening to take baths. Mum tried tactfully to reform him, by buying him men's toiletries and new clothes, but it was all a waste of time. He left after a couple of nights, taking Dad's new mobile phone with him.

Dad is usually pretty laid back and tolerant of Mum's ideas and projects, both of them having been hippie types themselves back in their youth. They'd met at Glastonbury when they were both eco-warriors. But the smelly man was a bit too much, in his opinion.

"I think it would be nice to have Christmas with just us and the kids," he said the following year.

"But it seems so selfish," said Mum. "We have so much, and there are so many with next to nothing. And Christmas is a time for giving and sharing."

Mum had her way, of course. That year we'd had a foreign student who couldn't afford to travel home for Christmas, and an old lady she'd met in the Post Office, who was all on her own. This year we were having Granddad.

Granddad and Grandma had spent several Christmases with us over the years, and other times during the year as well. We went to their house a lot too. I loved being with them, because when I was little I was the only grandchild and they made a big fuss of me. But it was still fun when Rowan came along too, and got big enough to join in things. Grandma taught us both to cook, because Mum is an artist and she isn't the best cook in the world. Mum's efforts as often as not turn out to be either burnt or half-cooked, stuck to the pan or running off the plate. Maybe I exaggerate, she does manage to feed us, but let's just say that cooking, and especially fancy cooking, is not her forte. Grandma taught us how to cook eggs a dozen different ways, to grill chops and prepare veg and to make all kinds of cakes. She also took us raspberry picking and blackberrying and mushroom gathering, and we made jams and jellies, pickles and soups, together. It's probably due to Grandma that we're not seriously malnourished, Rowan and I. And she read us stories, all three cuddled up together in her big comfy armchair.

My dad is a teacher, and Granddad had been a teacher too. He had taught sciences and natural history, and loved the natural world, especially trees and anything to do with wood. Come to think of it, this interest in trees must be a family thing. Mum and Dad once chained themselves to trees to stop them being cut down, and they gave us these embarrassing tree names. And, thinking of it, the amazing thing is that Jay has this passion for trees too. Jay is American, he is gorgeous, and he's a few years older than me. The girls think he's my boyfriend, but I tell them he's just a good friend who happens to be a boy. But, deep down, I think he will be my boyfriend one day. We'll see . . .

Anyway, Granddad taught us about the different kinds of wood, and showed us lots of things we could do with wood. We helped him cut hazel poles to support the beans in his vegetable garden and carry them home. Then, with the ones left over, he showed us how to put them into a circle, binding them together at the top to make a tepee or wigwam. We made whistles and blowpipes of hollow elder stems. He helped us make bows and arrows, and shoot them at a target fastened to one of the apple trees. Grandma confiscated the bows and arrows after we accidentally shot one of the neighbour's chickens. It wasn't badly hurt, but very upset, and stopped laying for a while, which made the neighbour cross. Granddad thought it might be better if we stuck to something safer for a while, so we made rafts of sticks lashed together with string and sailed them on a pool we made by damming the stream.

But all these good times are just memories now, back in the past, and we were all very sad about it. Grandma died about two years ago, very suddenly, of a heart attack, after just putting the last label on a batch of damson jam. Mum tried to comfort us by saying that it was the way Grandma would have wanted to go, but I didn't want her to go at all, and cried buckets. Granddad suddenly seemed as though all the life had gone out of him too, he sat indoors and neglected his garden and didn't eat properly. Then he picked up a bit and seemed better. But it wasn't long before we all noticed how increasingly forgetful he was. He forgot to feed the cat so often that it left home and went to live with the neighbour at the end of the road. Sometimes we suspected he forgot to feed himself. But it was only when he started doing things like putting the milk and butter into the oven instead of the fridge, or going out in one shoe and one slipper, that Mum and Dad got really worried. Granddad had lost the plot.

"Something will have to be done," I heard them say to each other more than once.

When Granddad let a pan boil dry and caused a small

fire, and then burnt his hand trying to put it out, they decided action must be taken immediately. Mum and Dad tried to get Granddad to live with us, but he point blank refused. He didn't want to be a burden to us young people, he said (meaning Mum and Dad too!). But he couldn't go on living alone, so in the end he agreed to go into a residential home with a special unit for people with dementia. I cried again. It was almost as bad as when Grandma died. We'd lost her, and now we'd lost the Granddad we knew as well. He was there, but not the same person.

And now he was coming for Christmas.

"Are you sure about this?" asked Dad worriedly. Granddad was his father, and he wasn't at all sure Mum could manage with him in the house. I could see his point. Mum is absent-minded at the best of times. Would she cope with an elderly man even more so, who sometimes didn't even remember who we were?

"It's Christmas," said Mum, as if that settled everything. "People need to be with their families at Christmas. He can't spend it with a lot of old people sitting round wearing silly hats and having sing-songs. He'd hate it. He'll come to us."

two

Granddad came to us a week or so before Christmas, to get settled in. He'd always been a tall man, but seemed more stooped than I remembered and not as tall. Or maybe I'd grown in the last year or so. When he removed his peaked cap, his hair was whiter. Granddad was always a perfect gentleman and still remembered the manners he'd been taught, like removing headgear in the house and standing up when a lady entered the room. I wondered if he did that in the Home. There'd be an awful lot of getting up and sitting down if so, with all the nurses and carers running around.

He looked pleased to see us, if a little confused. I gave him a big hug, and he hugged me back and said, "You're looking well. It's so nice to see you again, Harriet."

I knew that Harriet had been Granddad's older sister. My dad had told me about her. The red hair in our family comes from Dad's side. He and Rowan both have sandy-brown hair, but mine is flaming red, and apparently Harriet's had been, too.

I said, "It's me, Granddad. It's Willow."

He looked thoughtful, and then said, "Willow is

such a pretty name. I have a little granddaughter called Willow."

I felt tears come to my eyes and turned my head away. Mum touched my hand and said quietly, "Better just to humour him, love. If people try to correct him it seems to make him more confused."

It was hard, though, remembering how Granddad had been before. Physically he was still quite fit, he could get about and liked to go for walks. On his first morning with us, a Saturday, he suggested going to the park.

"But there's snow on the ground, Dad," said my dad. "It's very cold out, and the pavements might be a bit slippery."

Granddad snorted. "A bit of cold weather never hurt anyone. I like to be out in the fresh air. I'll take Willow and Rowan for a walk."

Granddad seemed much better this morning. He was even remembering about the park in town, and was getting our names right. Maybe he wasn't as bad as we'd thought. It would take us a day or two to realise that his illness followed a pattern, and that there was gradual deterioration as the day went by.

I said quickly, "That's a good idea. I have my Saturday job to do first, but then we can take you – I mean, you can take us, for a walk in the park, Granddad."

When I got back at lunch time I could see that Mum had that frazzled expression that told us she'd had a difficult morning, or even wondered if she'd bitten off more than she could chew. Getting lunch in the kitchen, she muttered that she'd had an awful job of it to keep Granddad from trying to light the electric fire with matches or help her put the crockery away in all the wrong places. Dad had needed to go into school to pick up some papers, Rowan had gone round to Harry's, and she was feeling the strain.

In the end, she'd found a piece of wood and a penknife and sat Granddad down to whittle, which kept him occupied for quite a while.

"It was the bluntest I could find, and I just prayed he wouldn't do himself any kind of mischief," she said.

"Poor Granddad," I said.

"I must say he seems happier when you children are about," she said. "It seems to settle him. Will you be OK with him this afternoon?"

"We'll be fine," I said.

Getting Granddad ready to go out was just like dressing a child, I thought, watching Mum fussing. He thought that all he needed was his peaked cap and a long scarf round his neck – his 'muffler' as he called it. We had a struggle to get him to put on his thick coat, and then he buttoned it up crookedly and we had to do it all over again. Then we had to track down his gloves. Mum had a look of profound relief on her face when we were all ready, and practically shoved us out of the door.

"Don't stand about getting cold," she said. "But on the other hand, no need to hurry back. Maybe you could get a coffee at that little place on the corner."

Granddad seemed much happier out of doors and more

like his old self. He pointed out the shapes of the trees
standing leafless and bare against the wintry background,
and told us about the sap going down to nourish the
roots in winter and rising to produce shoots and leaves
when spring came again. I guessed it would have been
interesting to be in his class during his teaching days,
and felt a rush of pity for the way his life had changed.
It's cruel, I thought, and wondered why God allowed
things like that to happen. I tucked my hand through his
arm, and Rowan held his hand on the other side.

We went to the park, where a gaggle of ducks had
come to try and swim on the pond, and found only a
sheet of ice. They were slipping and slithering about,
looking in vain for their familiar water, and quacking in
bewilderment. Even Granddad couldn't help chuckling
at their antics, and it was a good sound to hear.

"It's cold," said Rowan after a bit. His nose had turned
pink, and I noticed that Granddad's face had a bit of a
blue tinge. We went to the coffee shop on the corner to
warm up, and I ordered hot chocolate for the three of us.
Granddad and Rowan both blew on theirs to cool it. The
two of them were getting on like a house on fire.

Granddad had been talking to us so sensibly all
afternoon that I wondered again whether everyone might
have been mistaken about his condition. It was when we
were starting for home that trouble loomed.

"Time we went home," said Granddad as we left the
café.

"Yes, we're going there now Granddad," I said.

But he seemed reluctant to take the direction we were headed for. "That's not the way home."

"It is, Granddad." Rowan and I were each side of him, trying to steer him in the right direction, but he was trying to pull the other way.

"I live in Newthorpe," he said. "Hazel Cottage, Newthorpe. That's my address."

"Not any more, Granddad," I said. "You're staying with us, at our house. For Christmas. We're going home now."

Rowan was getting impatient, hopping from foot to foot. "I need the toilet. And I'm cold."

"Stop complaining, Stanley," said Granddad. My heart sank. Stanley had been Granddad's younger brother. He was off in his own little world again.

I remembered Josh and Abi, and the tactics we'd resorted to. "It's nearly teatime," I said. "Mum will be getting tea ready. It's er – maybe it's muffins. With jam. Or hot buttered toast."

This was a shot in the dark, pure guesswork as to what Granddad might have had for tea in his childhood. It worked though. He brightened up and seemed eager to be off. "There might be dripping on the toast! Well, don't let's stand about in the cold. Let's go. Come along, Harriet. I'm hungry."

three

Granddad came to church with me on Sunday morning. My parents are not churchgoers, so it was strange to be sitting with a family member instead of with my mates. Granddad looked very dapper in his best suit, with his white hair neatly brushed. And he sang all the Advent hymns with great gusto, from memory because he'd forgotten his glasses, word perfect and never missing a beat. I was surprised, until I remembered that he and Granny used to take Rowan and me to the church in their village when we'd stayed with them. Fortunately he'd remembered his hearing aid, and listened intently to the sermon and the rest of the service.

There was coffee in the vestry afterwards, more for the older people, which we don't usually stay for, but today I did, because I felt it was a kindness to Mum to stay out of the house as long as possible. She was making a valiant attempt to make Granddad feel welcome, keep an eye on him, and get ready for Christmas, all at once, and was finding it hard going.

Granddad was an instant hit with the church people, especially the older ladies. He was at his charming best, lucid and talkative, and soon had an interested audience of old dears around him. I slipped over to chill with Sadie for a few minutes while he was occupied. She said, "He's a real sweetie, your granddad. Quite a charmer."

I agreed, but felt I must come clean about Granddad's true condition.

"Mornings he's usually good," I said. "But that changes, especially towards evening. He lives in a Home now, all the time. He has dementia."

I hated that word. It sounded as though Granddad was crazy, and he wasn't, just confused. But there was no kinder way of describing how he was. Losing his marbles? Bats in the belfry? One sandwich short of a picnic? Doolally? I'd heard all these labels and I wasn't attaching any of them to my granddad.

"Oh, I didn't realise," said Sadie. "That's sad." She looked really sorry, and I suddenly wanted to burst into tears and ask why God allowed things like this to happen to people.

Sadie sometimes joked that she needed to permanently wear a waterproof cape, because if it wasn't the babies dribbling and puking and wiping their noses on her, it was one of us girls shedding buckets of tears on her shoulder. Today she was wearing a rather chic velvety top, and I didn't want to be the one to ruin it, so I kept my cool. But I couldn't help saying, in a voice that sounded a bit choked, "I don't know why things like this happen to people like Granddad. I don't know why God allows it."

"Oh, honey," said Sadie, and reached out an arm to

me, which almost undid me. "It's just one of the things that happen in this sad world. People suffer, the lovely ones as well as the not so nice ones. Christians as well as those who don't believe. The big comfort is, Jesus knows about suffering and he helps us to bear it."

"But I don't even know how to behave to Granddad anymore," I said miserably. "Sometimes he's the person he used to be. Other times he's like a little kid. He even thinks he's one. He thinks I'm his big sister."

"You just have to love him," said Sadie gently. "Just keep on loving him. Don't try to work it all out. Asking questions won't get you far. Getting angry doesn't really help, although God can cope with our anger and doesn't hold it against us. Love is what each of us needs most. Just love your granddad, as he is."

I had no problem with that, I thought, walking home arm in arm with Granddad on a crisp, frosty morning with Christmas just round the corner. Granddad chatted about church and the people there, he'd had a great morning. I told him about our play, which was less than a week away now. And when we got home we found that Mum and Dad between them had cooked a roast beef dinner, with Yorkshire puds and all the trimmings, and that it was pretty much perfectly done. I felt that things were not so bad after all. Especially as Mum had had a peaceful morning and was looking more relaxed and less frazzled.

But nothing stays the same for long. There were only two days of school left, and therefore only two more sessions of Beech Bank. I didn't want to miss them, so it was six thirty when I got home next day. Rowan appeared to be alone in the house, eating bread and butter and maple syrup in front of the TV. There was no smell of anything cooking and apparently no one else about.

"Where is everyone?"

"Gone to see one of the other mums, I think," said Rowan, licking syrup from his fingers. I shuddered. There'd be sticky patches on the sofa cushions, I knew.

"Granddad too? Whatever for?"

"I think Justin's mum was worried about something."

"What do you mean?"

"Well, Granddad escaped this afternoon and came to the school to meet me. We walked home together, it was nice. But Justin's mum was worried and rang up, and now they've gone to explain."

My heart sank. I could picture all too well what had happened. A parent had panicked when she saw Rowan going off with someone she didn't know. Why didn't she have the sense to speak to Rowan, I wondered?

Mum was hopping mad when the three of them got home, but with Justin's mum and not with Granddad.

"Stupid woman!" she fumed, banging saucepans about in the kitchen. "Jumping to conclusions. Thank goodness she didn't phone the police! She even told me Rowan is too young to be walking home on his own – she'd never dream of letting her Justin do that! I told her I was bringing up my children to be independent and think for themselves."

I felt a wild desire to giggle. "And *we* had to apologise to *her*, and explain about Granddad," she went on. "Poor old fellow, he hadn't a clue about what was going on. Just kept saying he'd gone to meet Stanley after school."

I looked through into the lounge, where Dad was setting out the chess pieces for a game with Granddad. He could still play, after a fashion, though he called the rooks crows and the knights horses. I went through and sat on the arm of his chair and gave him a hug. He said, "Oh, there you are, Harriet. Have you had a good day? I did, until we went to visit that woman who looked as though she'd just sucked a lemon! I didn't like her much. It's nice to be home again."

four

Christmas was almost here, with preparations well under way in our house. Not that there was much organisation to speak of. My mother is not an organised person. But we had the tree up and decorated, twinkling lights trailing round mirrors and banisters, shopping more or less done and food in the freezer. Rows of bright Christmas cards were strung up and Mum was panicking about the people she'd forgotten to send one to. Dad was mildly fuming about the number of times he had to fiddle with tree lights when they blew fuses, and about the extra expense of Christmas in general. It was all pretty normal.

Mum might not be organised generally, but she has the most wonderful talent for wrapping presents. I suppose it's her artistic gifting. No presents bundled up hastily in holly wrapping paper with a stick-on tag for her. She does hers up in the most beautiful gold or silver or shiny purple wrapping, like luscious chocs in a box, with satin ribbon and twirly streamers and rosettes, and labels in elegant handwriting and little hand-drawn motifs. They make your mouth water to look at them, and at the same time you don't want to spoil them by tearing them open. There were a pile of these gathering under the Christmas tree, and Rowan was sorely tempted to pick little holes in the corners to try and see what was inside.

And now Christmas was only a few days away, and the day of the Nativity play had come. All of us were going, even Granddad (or especially Granddad, who loved everything to do with special performances at school or church), and most of us at BB were in a fever of anticipation. I was one of the angels; all we had to do was stand quietly around the sides of the darkened hall, and at the right moment, burst into a chorus of praise and adoration.

My mum might be wonderful with present wrapping and tree decoration, but her talents did not extend to dressmaking. So Annie's mum had offered to do mine along with Annie's. They were to be simple white robes, wide and gathered from the neck, like a vicar's surplice.

Sadie must have got the idea from Rod's. When we stood with folded hands, the robes draped around us, when we raised our arms in worship they would look like wings. Or that was the idea. We hadn't had a dress rehearsal, or any kind of rehearsal for that matter. It was all to be spontaneous, Sadie said. My dad said he'd helped to produce many school plays in his time, and spontaneous could be very tricky.

The play was to be at 5pm, no later because it was still cold and wintry, and people would not want to be out and about late. The outside bit would be over in 15 or 20 minutes, the donkey transported safely home in a horse box, and the rest would happen in the Beech Bank club headquarters. Chairs had been set out for the audience earlier that day, and a few props prepared.

I'd arranged to be at Annie's good and early to try on the finished robes, make any necessary last-minute adjustments, and then to get to BB in good time. I was all ready to go, when my phone buzzed, and a number came up that made my heart flip.

"Jay!"

"Hey there! How you doin', Willow?"

It was so lovely to hear his voice, hundreds of miles away but sounding as though he was in the next room. I could picture his smile and the lock of hair that flopped over his forehead. We don't speak often, it's just too expensive, and we mostly stick to Chatspace or Skype. There was no way I was going to miss out on talking to him. I'd just have to hurry afterwards, maybe miss trying on the robe. I was sure it would be fine.

I'm not sure how long we chatted, but the time seemed to fly by. I could have talked longer but I had to go, explaining why. I was really cutting it fine now. I hurried to Annie's and found her looking a bit anxious.

"I thought something had happened. Your phone was engaged for ages."

"Yes, sorry," I said. "Jay."

"Ah." She needed no further explanation. She was hurrying me, pulling out my angel robe and throwing it over my head almost before I'd got my coat off.

"No time to change properly, we'll just have to see how it looks over your clothes for now."

I couldn't believe it, but before we could even look in the mirror the phone buzzed again. Annie is pretty cool usually, but she was beginning to look flustered.

"If it's him wanting to talk more, tell him no chance!"

It wasn't Jay. It was Mum. They'd lost Granddad again.

"Lost him?"

"Yes, he must have taken it into his head to set off without waiting for us."

"Oh my goodness! Have you looked for him?"

"Of course we have!" Mum sounded a bit short-tempered. "I'm asking you to keep a lookout too. Goodness knows where he's wandered off to."

"We'll have to hurry!" said Annie. "Let's have a look at you."

The last thing I wanted was to let Sadie and the others down. They'd worked so hard. Yet I thought about Granddad, more confused as the day wore on, wandering the dark streets in a place he wasn't used to, after dark, with slippery patches still in some places. If he fell with nobody about . . . It didn't bear thinking about.

"You go on," I said. "I'll come as soon as I can. I've got to look for Granddad."

"But . . ." I didn't wait for her to finish. I was out of the room and down the stairs, still in my angel robe, gathering up its folds in one hand as I ran.

I was trying desperately to think where Granddad might head for. He knew the school and the church and some of the shops. I ran in the direction of Rowan's school, but could see it was all in darkness. The looming building of the church at the end of the street was all dark too. I headed for the town centre.

Most of the shops were closed and I was surprised to see so many people still about. Folk were mostly at home by this time, having their tea or watching TV. Then I saw that some were dressed in long dark robes and Arab headgear and remembered that these were meant to be the travellers thronging Bethlehem to pay their taxes. Others were ordinary people from town who had come out to watch the proceedings. I bumped into Tony, one of the boys from Beech Bank, who had what looked like his mother's tablecloth on his head. He did a double take when he saw me. "Willow?"

I didn't think I looked much odder than he did, but

then caught a sudden glimpse of my reflection in a plate glass window. Long white robe, red hair standing out like some wild halo round my head, staring eyes. If I looked like an angel, it was a crazy, avenging kind of one. No wonder a few people had looked oddly at me.

"Aren't you supposed to be at BB?" he asked.

"I'm looking for my granddad," I said, and hurried on, peering into people's faces under the street lighting.

Then suddenly, all the street lights went out. There was a surprised gasp and some murmuring from the people milling around. A few of the houses in the main street had dim lights shining from their windows, as arranged. I could hardly see anything now, people's faces looked shadowed and mysterious. Where on earth was Granddad?

And then an expectant hush seemed to come over the crowd. All eyes were turned towards the junction where the main street was crossed by another, and next moment we heard the clip clop of hooves on the hard surface of the road.

five

A weary little group of travellers came round the corner. Even the donkey looked tired, head drooping, feet plodding resignedly as though he'd covered many miles. He was led by a tall young man in winter robes, stooping a little but careful of the young girl on the donkey's back, who swayed wearily and held on tight to the saddle. A murmur ran round the crowds in the street. An event of great significance was unfolding before their eyes.

I felt rooted to the spot, watching with the others as the young man turned the donkey towards the door of the Blue Boar Inn on the corner. He knocked. A man answered the door, a man in Eastern clothing and headcovering. No words were spoken. The young man indicated the drooping donkey, the weary girl. The innkeeper shrugged, shook his head, spread his hands wide in a helpless gesture, closed the door. No room. The young man returned to the donkey, touching the girl's shoulder briefly, led the donkey up the street towards another inn. Some of the people followed.

I came to my senses. I still hadn't found Granddad. Then, suddenly, my head seemed to clear and the panic died. Had anyone thought to check Beech Bank, to see if Granddad had arrived there safely as planned? Or had we all, including me, assumed that he would be wandering aimlessly somewhere around town? It could be that he'd been at BB all the time.

"Numpty!" I said aloud, and turned to hurry through the little alley between the shops that would lead me out into Beech Bank. It was still dark as I went down the hill, but the lights were on at the BB headquarters and there were lots of cars in the park. I dived through the door into a world of warmth and light, and people scurrying about. There was a buzz of talk from the big hall, where the audience was already assembling. I opened the small side door a crack and peeped through, scanning the rows of chairs, and, yes, there was a familiar white head in a row about half-way down, sitting at the end. I felt a rush of relief, tinged with a tiny hint of irritation. He'd been here all the time, while the rest of us were going frantic with worry about him. I reached for my phone to text Mum and tell her, and found there was a text message there already. "G'dad at BB. All OK." I hadn't heard the bleep. I'd been too busy running around. "Numpty!" I said again.

Annie suddenly appeared, wearing her angel robe and looking flustered.

"There you are! Hurry up! We're supposed to be in our places."

There was no time to change properly and tidy up. I pulled a face I liked to be perfectly dressed and groomed when I went out, and now here I was on the big night, crumpled robe, messy hair, everything in disarray. Well, it couldn't be helped.

The lights dimmed as I went into the hall, and a hush fell. I scuttled into a place against the wall near the door. All around the room white figures were standing silent in the shadows, heads down, hands clasped, waiting. Amber, who was nearest to me, said in a whisper, "What happened to you? Where've you been?"

There was no time to explain now. "Later," I whispered back.

The hall was hushed in the dim light, even the children in the audience had fallen silent. There was a hint of movement on the stage. Then a soft light went on at the back and we saw a simple scene, a few hay bales, the young girl sitting on one holding a baby, the young man moving quietly about. The girl was wrapping the baby, swaddling it in yards and yards of white material. The young man went aside and came back carrying a small wooden feeding trough. He loosened some hay and filled the trough with it, then pulled a garment, maybe a cloak, from a saddlebag and placed it on top of the hay, making a soft lining. The young mother tenderly laid her swaddled baby into the makeshift crib and sat down again beside it. The young man fetched a blanket from the saddlebag and wrapped it around her shoulders against the cold of the night. Both of them gazed at the sleeping child, their faces alight with love and wonder.

All this was done in silence, and I jumped when an amplified voice – Rod's – sounded from the darkness at the back of the stage, reading from the book of Isaiah in the Bible:

For to us a child is born, to us a son is given, and the government will be on his shoulders. And he will be called Wonderful Counsellor, Mighty God, Everlasting Father, Prince of Peace.

His voice died away. There was silence for a moment, you could have heard a pin drop in the hall. We waited for our cue from Sadie, which would signal a blaze of light from all over the hall, while at the same moment we angels would step forward, lift our heads, raise our arms and sing a song of praise and worship: "Hark! The herald angels sing: Glory to the new-born King!" The congregation would join in the second verse, then there would be more readings and carols telling the Christmas story.

That was the plan. But it didn't quite happen like that.

Before Sadie could give us the cue signal, one of the small children in the audience, maybe one who'd been in a Nativity play himself and felt the lack of shepherds and wise men, left his seat, trotted to the front and climbed the steps to the stage. In one hand he clutched a tatty looking stuffed rabbit. This he laid down at the foot of the manger. Then he stood, looking down at the sleeping baby. Next moment, a little girl got up and joined him, and then it seemed that all the small children were leaving their seats and going forward to the stage. A few had toys with them, teddies or cuddly dogs, and one little boy had a red plastic tractor. These they laid down beside the crib, their gifts to the baby born to be king. Then one child knelt down, still facing the manger, and one by one the others followed, kneeling quietly. I heard sniffles from the audience, and saw eyes being dabbed with tissues. My own eyes were wet.

And then the most amazing thing of all happened. A tall figure rose from his seat at the end of a row and joined the children on the stage, creakily bending his knees and kneeling amongst them. The soft light shone on his white head.

I wondered how Rod and Sadie would deal with this unrehearsed aberration from their planned event. They'd wanted spontaneous but maybe this was going a bit far. Would Rod tactfully persuade Granddad to return to his seat, and indicate that the mums should gather up their offspring?

But none of this happened. Instead, Rod did what the baby in the manger would himself do when he became a man and began his ministry on earth. While we all held our breaths in expectation, he came from the back of the stage and moved among the children, laying his hand on each small head, praying and asking a blessing on each one. When he reached my granddad he didn't hesitate for a moment, but laid a hand on his white head and blessed him too.

And suddenly the tears were running down my cheeks and I felt this love welling up inside me, love for the watching people in the audience, love for my family, my friends, and love for my granddad which swallowed up every trace of the irritation I had felt. Because God loved us all, the young and the old, the rich and the poor, those who were beginning their lives with high hopes, and those like my granddad who had been strong and capable and now were reduced again to the status of little children.

He loved us so much that he had sent his only son to be born into our world as a helpless baby, to live and work and show the love of God to all he met, and by his death to make the sacrifice for us all that would gain for us freedom and forgiveness and everlasting life.

Then the music started and we sang, "*Glory to the new-born King*".

For maybe the first time in my life, I was experiencing the true meaning of Christmas.

If you would like to talk to the author about any of the issues raised in this book, you may contact her by emailing meckade@hotmail.com, or by post to:

Eleanor Watkins
c/o Dernier Publishing
P.O. Box 403
Tonbridge
TN9 9BJ
UK

Or use the contact form on our website:
www.dernierpublishing.com

Beech Bank Girls II – Making a Difference

Not long after Chloe's party (*Beech Bank Girls – Every Girl Has A Story*), the Beech Bank Girls are back! Holly is in Australia, but Willow, Amber, Chloe, Annie and Rachel discover that they do not have to wait until their gap year to start helping people in need. An interesting hike, a new culture on their doorstep, an emotional evening . . . the friends learn from some tough issues that they can make a difference right where they are and have lots of fun at the same time!

"A very exciting, fun to read, really well-written and easy to understand book. Looking forward to the next one!"
– Taylor

"When the girls get into bad situations or dilemmas, they all get together and pray . . . makes you want to read more and find out what happens next."   – Ellie

"A great story."   – Eleanor

ISBN: 978 0 9536963 7 6

Also available from Dernier Publishing for 8–11s:

I Want to Be an Airline Pilot
by Mary Weeks Millard

Shema, a Rwandan goatherd from a child-led family, has many adventures, including a goat eating his T-shirt and a close brush with a spitting black cobra! Although he is an orphan, he discovers that he has a Father in heaven who cares for him.

> "This book made me feel happy, sad and really excited . . . it is one of my favourites."
> – Kemi

ISBN 978 0 9536963 5 2

Living in Hope
by Mary Weeks Millard

Shema can now go to school and his dream of becoming an airline pilot has moved one step closer – but he and his family and friends still have many exciting and dangerous challenges to face in the Village of Hope. The thrilling sequel to *I Want to Be an Airline Pilot*, set in rural Rwanda.

> "A brilliant, riveting story."
> – Reuben

ISBN 978 0 9569043 0 0

The Birthday Shoes
by Mary Weeks Millard

Emily Jane hates her new shoes until she finds that they hold an amazing secret! Join her as she goes on magical journeys to Africa, making new friends and some exciting discoveries about God.

> "My favourite part was when Emily Jane put on her shoes for the first time and ended up in Africa. It made me feel like I was there!"　　　　　　　　　　　　　　　　– Susanna

ISBN 978 0 9536963 8 3

Deepest Darkness
by Denise Hayward

Ten-year-old Abi suffers from terrible nightmares and her life is ruled by fear. On holiday in Canada, she makes a new friend who shows her through a series of adventures that true light shines, even in the deepest darkness.

> "This is a brilliant story . . . one of the best books I have read – EVER!"　　　　　　　　　　　　　　　　　– Maddie

ISBN 978 0 9536963 6 9

Books for 12s+:

The Only Way by Gareth Rowe

When a miserable, disaffected teenager meets the beautiful and mysterious Lily, he discovers a new way to live, the only way. Later, when Lily's life is in danger, he is willing to risk everything to save her, but time and circumstances are against him.

> "*The Only Way* is a moving, fast-paced, gripping and genius piece of writing."
>
> – G. P. Taylor, *New York Times*' best-selling author of *Shadowmancer*

ISBN 978 0 9536963 9 0

London's Gone by J. M. Evans

London has been bombed by terrorists. Now Maria must make a hazardous journey to safety with her sister and a Christian friend. For Maria, the journey is also inside herself as she begins to discover a side to life that she did not know existed. A thrilling drama full of suspense.

> "I found the story very tense and compelling." – Sandy

ISBN 978 0 9536963 2 1

All our books are available from your local bookshop, on-line book store or directly from www.dernierpublishing.com